THE
DINGLEMEN
ON COURSE

This novel is a work of fiction. Names, characters, places, and incidents are either the product of the author's imagination or used fictitiously. Any resemblance to actual events, locales, organisations, or persons, living or dead, is entirely coincidental and beyond the intent of either the author or publisher.

CHAPTER ONE

Clever thought he was too dignified to scurry, but that's exactly what he was doing, scurrying through the tunnels as if he was a cheese-addicted rat. He grimaced, hating to be late, especially for this gathering with the Dingledell elders. In his mad rush he bounced around a corner, whacking a shoulder into the opposite tunnel wall where the wood was worn smooth by generations of Dinglemen doing exactly the same manoeuvre. He rubbed his shoulder as he hurtled his way towards the gathering, muttering that it would be nice if he could get there without requiring medical attention.

Clever finally eased his way through the cavern doorway, grateful for cover behind the backs of larger Dinglemen, and heaved a sigh of relief. He would hate for anyone to think that he could ever be tardy, but by all appearances he might have gotten away with sneaking in.

"Ah, Clever! So! You have chosen to join us," boomed a voice from somewhere in the centre of the cavern. Clever sighed and forced back the urge to roll his eyes. He could feel his face flushing a beet-red, but he drew in a deep breath, puffed out a scrawny chest, and stepped forward through the grinning faces surrounding him. The Dinglemen at the rear shuffled aside to let him wriggle through until he stood before the elders seated on the raised platform at the centre of the gathering. He nodded towards them, trying to be as formal as he could, while ignoring the smirking of those around him. The tiny elder on the speaker's pillar spoke slowly and deliberately.

"We have considered and assigned," he said.

Clever warily eyed the speaker. It always annoyed him that this wise, ancient leader only gave out little-bitty pieces of information each time he spoke.

"He presides over the whole of Dingledell," Clever muttered to himself, "and can't even string a full sentence together."

The elder looked amused.

"Patience, Clever. You will be informed soon enough."

Clever winced, wondering if the elder had guessed what he was thinking. He really needed to work on his bland face. The elder lifted his head and scanned the upturned faces with pale grey eyes and a suddenly serious expression.

"Most have heard. An injury was just missed."

Clever felt his face flush again and his ears burn with embarrassment. He was never going to live it down. And it wasn't even his fault! How was he to know he was being followed by that inkblot on his last expedition? Sure, the humans were much closer than ever before, but that had been a good thing. He had been learning so much! And there was no danger really. Nimin was fine, wasn't he? So what was the fuss about? And now, he, Clever, was going to be known as being both irresponsible and tardy. Arggh, the shame!

"Our forest is no longer ours. We must leave," the tiny elder stated simply, to a loud collective gasp. Clever blinked, speechless, while the elder smiled a sad smile in his direction. "There is no fault. The humans are here."

Clever couldn't help but stare. He had been enjoying not having to hike too far to observe what the humans were doing, not having to carry so much equipment with him, or having to spend his precious time preparing for big trips. He had been amazed as he watched the way the massive machines had torn away great chunks of earth and scraped away every tree and bush in their path. But surely they weren't that close, were they? Clever glanced around at the shocked faces behind him. They were standing in a cavern where generations of Dinglemen had stood, where generations had gathered. He could see the same thought on every face. This was Dingledell. It was their home, where their food was cooked, their jokes were played and their stories were told. And hadn't it been their home for as long as memory itself? A furious buzzing swelled as the Dinglemen started to whisper to their neighbours. The elder cast his gaze around the room to hush the crowd before he continued, spreading his arms wide as he spoke.

"Young Dinglemen do not remember. This place of ours is not Dingledell."

"What?! Er, I mean, pardon me, but look here, not–?" said Clever.

"This *place* is not Dingledell."

Clever couldn't help looking squiggle-eyed at the elder. Not Dingledell? He risked another glance at all of the boggling eyes and open mouths.

"There has been no need to tell. You will hear."

The elder motioned forward a portly Dingleman from the semi-circle behind him, who shuffled to the front of the platform and cleared his throat.

"This is the story of our beginning," he began ponderously, sounding as if he was reading the words from an unfurled and very dusty scroll. "At the dawn of our time, we were known to the humans. But we were betrayed for sport and for gain." He paused and coughed, then raised his eyes to check that everyone was listening. He continued. "We learned that the humans are dangerous. We decided that Dingledell must only exist in hearts and heads, so that our home may never be destroyed. And so we chose to follow and to watch, to know the human tongues and to learn their ways. We now carry Dingledell in hearts and heads. This is the story of our beginning."

Clever couldn't quite suppress a smirk. He had known his research was important, and he had known the elders had encouraged his interest in the humans, but he had never realised just how valuable his efforts were. The ancient elder nodded once and gestured the portly Dingleman back into his place.

"We will find a new home. The next Dingledell." The elder raised a finger for attention. "We will not run. We will always be followed if we run."

The whole chamber was silent, despite the number of Dinglemen within the walls of the great cavern. Normally, there was the sound of shuffling feet or hasty whisperings, but now all ears were strained open, all bodies completely still.

"We will move to the human city. The human city has parks. Protected areas."

There was a stunned silence, and then the cavern exploded into babbled noise. Once again the elder raised a hand. Clever found himself taking in tiny irrelevant details while his shocked mind refused to digest this news. He wondered why the elder's hand was smooth and unwrinkled, when his face looked like glaciers had spent the last few centuries carving deep folds beneath his eyes and alongside his nose. And, Clever noticed, the elder on the end, the one who was always nodding off during gatherings, had done just that. His eyes were closed and his drowsing chin was firmly planted on his chest.

"Protected areas with trees," the elder on the pillar said loudly, noting where Clever was looking. Clever watched the end elder snort awake, blinking at finding himself on the raised platform and in the middle of something important. Clever tried to shift his attention back to what was being said.

"We will follow our beginning. We will move Dingledell in the direction of the humans."

Clever felt numb, and he wasn't sure if it was because moving to a human city was an inspired idea or because the shock hadn't sunk in yet. He thought, perhaps, yes. Perhaps it was a good idea. Their home would not be built over because the city would already be built. And he was good at watching humans. He felt himself start to smile and he nodded thoughtfully. How wise of the elders to think of that.

"Clever, you have researched humans," the elder said. Clever nodded in agreement.

"You understand them."

Clever wasn't too sure about this but he nodded anyway.

"You are intelligent." He nodded agreement again and detected a ripple of a groan passing around the cavern.

"You will lead."

Clever's heart immediately leapt in his chest. Oh no, not him! He wasn't some adventurer. He was a scientist! Once again the elder smiled, as if he was reading Clever's mind and was now enjoying his dismay.

"You will have help. Choose."

Clever sighed, well aware he wouldn't be able to wriggle out of the assignment now the elders had made and announced their decision. Besides, he thought, trying to convince himself, he did know the most about humans, and he would get the opportunity to learn more about them if he was living in one of their protected parks. That thought made him feel slightly better. He narrowed his eyes while he considered his options. Firstly, given the near incident on his last trip – the one that wasn't his fault – he should take along a guard for protection. There was no question about who was best designed for that appointment. In fact, Clever saw, he didn't even need to say who he wanted to take with him. Sarge was already muscling his way forward to stand at his side. Clever just tilted his head towards Sarge. He could have sworn he detected a flicker of a smile in response.

"Certainly. You may take Sarge."

"And Weebit," Clever said. He would need the genius architect once they found a suitable place for their new home. There wasn't a better craftsman than Weebit.

"Acceptable. You may take Weebit."

Once again, Clever was sure he saw the edges of Sarge's mouth flicker and the tiniest nod of approval. Well, I'm glad you approve, you muscled up walnut, Clever thought to himself. A small Dingleman, with a shock of bright red hair, wiggled forward to stand next to Sarge.

"Prosper in your assignment," said the elder, folding his hands together and bowing his head at Clever and then in the direction of Sarge and Weebit. The other elders nodded and smiled and prodded the end elder awake, preparing for the gathering to break up. It was at that moment that there was a commotion near the tunnel entrance at the rear. A short, tubby Dingleman who was standing in the doorway, in trying to see what was happening, had lost his balance and tumbled into the Dingleman in front of him. That Dingleman had been pushed sideways, and a domino effect had resulted in a group of bodies crashing to the ground, while those far enough away just managed to sidestep to save themselves from a fall. The red-faced perpetrator succeeded in keeping his feet but was surrounded by a whining pile of cranky neighbours.

"Ah, Nimin. You choose to volunteer."

Clever shot a horrified glance at the elder, who smiled happily and nodded back at him. "To cook your food. It will keep you strong."

"Um, but—"

"Better to know he is with you, hmmm?"

Clever sighed. This was his punishment and it was a very high price. One look at Sarge's disgusted expression showed he felt the same way as Clever. Not only was Nimin young, clumsy, and in constant need of supervision, he was also under the illusion that he could cook. Clever thought of the last meal he had been offered by Nimin, some yellow gloop with sooty flecks all through it, and suppressed a shudder.

The elders indicated the end of the gathering. Dinglemen squeezed towards the tunnel in a muttering mass and Clever, Sarge and Weebit were left standing alone near the raised centre. The elders nodded at their chosen few before they minced down from the platform and swept out in a regal, dignified group. They glided past the embarrassed Nimin, and with the briefest of nods in his direction, were gone. There was a heavy pause, during which Clever and Sarge just stared at each other miserably, before Nimin piped up.

"Where are we going?"

#

Early the next morning, Clever met Sarge outside the entrance of Dingledell. The ground was slippy with moisture and he filled his lungs with pine-scented air, squinting through the branches above at the morning sun. At least it was going to be a beautiful day and he was glad they would be able to get away early. Who knew how long they would have to wait for a ride, or how long they would be travelling before they found somewhere to settle for the night. Weebit sidled up to stand silently behind Sarge, waiting patiently for them to move off.

They waited.

Several minutes later, Clever, blowing out his breath and tapping a foot, peered around Sarge's bulk to glare at Nimin. Nimin was struggling to drag an enormous backpack along the tunnel, finally pulling it to a laboured stop behind Weebit. Nimin wiped his face, fiddled with his pack, adjusted some of the contents, dropped a pot and retrieved it, stuffed it back on top, tightened the straps, scratched an itch on his leg and tugged his tunic into place, before finally looking up at Clever.

"Whut?"

Several more minutes passed before they finally set off, Nimin's backpack now light enough for him to carry. A huge pile of clothing, food and pots was left behind, dumped just inside the entrance.

#

Larry Gleghorn cursed under his breath and stabbed the brake pedal to the floor. His truck, with 'Breadalbone Forest Company' emblazoned on the drab grey sides, dribbled to a stop at the lights. He was hungry, in a hurry to get home to his dinner, and was daydreaming about bangers and mash with lots of gravy and mushy peas. Larry felt his stomach rumble and muttered again about the tyre. He should have been walking in his front door at home by now but had only just left the forest when the truck had started to handle badly. He'd had to pull over to check his tyres, finding a flat on the passenger rear side. Changing it had cost him over half an hour, and now he was stuck waiting at a traffic light.

Remembering that he'd put a roll of mints in the glove-box a few weeks ago, Larry stretched across the vinyl bench seat to search for them. He figured that mints were better than nothing. With his hand groping around at the back of the glove-box, and finding nothing but a soft potato chip and a bit of fluff, he thought he saw a quick flash of movement in the passenger side mirror. He blinked, peering into the smudged glass, but all he could see was a discarded burger container lying in the gutter near the rear wheel of his truck.

"Lazy kids, I'll bet, just littering for the sake of it," he muttered, feeling a bit better about having something else to complain about. "How hard would it be for them to put their rubbish in the bin? They just have no respect for the environment."

Finding the roll of mints in the ashtray, he gave a snort of triumph. He shovelled a couple into his mouth, and was glancing at the side mirror again when the car behind tooted impatiently to tell him the light was now green and could he, pretty please, get moving? Larry pushed the stick shift into first and trundled off across the intersection, leaving the car behind blanketed in a cloud of oily black smoke.

#

Several minutes passed until the road was quiet, and with no motorcars approaching Sarge carefully raised the lid of the burger container to peer out. Clever and Weebit lined up beside him, Clever scanning his eyes to the left and then swivelling them to the right, checking the road was clear in each direction. He turned to see what Nimin was doing, stifling a groan when he saw him poking at a rotten piece of greenery and then scratching at a large brown stain on the cardboard. Nimin sniffed at the stain, stood, and filled his lungs. "Oh, yeah. These humans know how to eat."

"Right, the coast is clear," said Sarge. He tugged his backpack higher onto his shoulders and shoved the container lid back.

"Let's move."

With Sarge leading, they hopped out of the container, quickly scaled the side of the concrete ditch, trotted across the short grass, and paused in front of a huge black wire fence. Clever squinted up, trying to see how high it was. He was aware of the sun hovering over the group of trees in the distance, and with the warmth of the day already fading the shadows cast by the fence were long and foreboding. He had the feeling the humans had been serious when they built this fence. It was made out of thick wire netting, with solid metal poles spaced along its length. Not just to keep animals out, thought Clever, but other humans as well. It was a formidable fence, one that nothing was supposed to penetrate. Well, except us of course, he corrected himself.

Twaanggg!

Sarge pushed his bag through one of the gaps in the netting and flipped through after it, caught his foot, twisted awkwardly and landed heavily on his back. He sprang to his feet, swore loudly and viciously kicked the pole that was nearby. Clever coughed to cover a smirk as Weebit and Nimin easily squirmed through after Sarge. Clever tested the wire and slipped through as elegantly as he could, then checked his finely woven feather-down tunic for stray particles of dirt. He liked his tunic. It was better than the khaki-coloured rough woven tunics the others wore with their rabbit-skin leggings and boots. Still, he liked being different, and who cared if they sniggered behind his back? He was the one with the brains. Wasn't he the one the elders had chosen to lead this assignment? Well, then. Although, if he could just work out how to keep the white tunic spotless he would be much happier.

They moved off across the short grass, heads rotating to take in the surroundings. Clever smiled at the clean expanse of tidy grounds, and his smile widened when he saw the surface of a small pond. It rippled gently, twinkling with silver and gold in the late afternoon light. Sarge strode out ahead of the others.

"Come on. Come on. This place looks fine. Let's find somewhere suitable and get cracking."

Clever glared at Sarge's back. Walnut! He was the one the elders had selected. He should be the one giving the orders. Except that Sarge looked like the order giving type he allowed, and he, Clever, looked like a scientist. Even the way Sarge walked said 'discipline'. Clever smiled to himself and ran with his thoughts. Or the way he walks says, 'my leggings are two sizes too small'. He snorted, receiving a blank stare from Sarge.

Nimin had spied the pond and raced towards it, shiny pots and pans falling out of his bag as he ran.

"Look, there's even fishes in the water!" He rubbed his hands together gleefully and turned around to grin at the others. Sarge surveyed the spilled cooking utensils with baleful eyes and muttered under his breath. While Clever agreed with Sarge about the pots, he decided he had better start acting like the leader, and the only way he could out-lead Sarge was to rely on his superior intelligence. Pretend he actually knew what he was doing.

"While I agree in principle with your initial conjecture, Nimin," he said pompously, "one must always proceed with caution when contemplating unfamiliar terrain." He mostly thought, ooh, that sounded very scholarly – but a small piece of his mind whispered 'schmuck'. He couldn't help it, though, it was the only weapon he had.

"Huh?"

Clever sighed.

"What I said was, the place looks all right, but I haven't seen trees spaced this way before. Look, they're in a row here," he said, and pointing through the trees, "and there's another row over there," and half-turning he pointed to another row in the opposite direction, "and over there." Clever frowned and stroked his chin, trying for what he hoped was an intellectual expression. "And then there are those wide strips of grass. I haven't seen humans lay out their grounds like this before is what I'm saying."

They all ignored Weebit as he walked up to the pond and peered through the ripples to see the fishes. Even from where Clever stood he could see flashes of orange, gold and silver as they swam in lazy circles near the water's edge. Clever kept musing about the unusual layout of trees until Weebit suddenly skidded forward on the soft ground and then wind-milled his arms wildly to catch his balance.

"We need shelter for the night, anyway," said Sarge, impassive as he watched Weebit flail. He nodded towards the far side of the grounds, behind two of the rows of trees.

"It looks like there's a promising bunch of woods over that way."

"You're absolutely correct," said Clever. He plucked a tiny blade of grass from his tunic, and he and Sarge watched patiently while Weebit still wobbled and wind-milled. He finally caught his balance and smiled an apology at them, before vaguely trailing after their rapidly departing backs. Nimin collected his pots and pans and hastily stuffed them into his bag, then lurched as fast as he could after the others.

"Wait!"

In minutes they had crossed the grass, with Clever wondering why it was cut to the same short length all the way from the road and the fence to the trees on the horizon. He was starting to feel excited about being able to spend some time determining the answer, and the answers to a lot more questions he had about the behaviour of humans. For example, why did they eat sparrow-grass? Yurghh. Why did they throw away words? Did the females wear powder on their faces to attract the males or was it really a form of disguise, or perhaps war-paint?

It was cooler under the pines, but there was still enough evening light to see as they walked and inspected the base of each tree in their path. Nimin spied a grub wriggling into the earth and bounded towards it across the pine-needled ground, returning with a big smile on his face, the grub hoisted up on his shoulder.

"Perfect! I can cook this for our dinner." He sniffed at the grub and wrinkled his nose. "Maybe with a few herbs."

Clever wondered if he was being too hard on the sparrow-grass. Sarge grimaced and glared across at the others.

"Weebit, what are you doing?"

Weebit was wandering off after a brightly coloured parrot, its vivid red and green feathers having caught his eye. The parrot was teasing him, moving from branch to branch while he walked blindly, often tripping on small roots as he kept his rapt attention fixed on the pretty bird. The parrot screeched laughter when Weebit disappeared from view near the roots of an imposing old tree. The others ran over and looked down into the hole into which Weebit had fallen.

"Now, that's want we want," said Sarge, "Well done, Weebit."

"Sterling effort," said Clever, not wanting to be outdone.

Nimin shoved his face right up into the entrance and peered inside at the cave formed under the tree, "ooh, that's maximal!"

Weebit sat up and wiped the dirt and cobwebs from his face. As he crawled back out, he was still looking up at the branches overhead for his parrot.

"All right, Weebit, no more fooling around," said Sarge, swinging his pack to the ground and waving a finger at the others to drop theirs. "Time for us to get to work."

Clever scowled and took his time dropping his bag.

#

Long after the sun had finally gone down and been replaced by a half-moon and stars, the sounds of sawing, hammering and bickering were fast driving Clever insane. He crawled out from under the tree to get away from the noise for a while. Sitting under a nearby tree, he gazed up through the branches, contemplating the surrounding woods, the fishes pond, and the orderly grass within the bounds of the fence. The cave's space extended farther within the root system than it appeared from the ground and he couldn't believe their luck in finding it on the first day. It was just like Weebit to stumble upon exactly what they needed, and Clever was glad he had had the foresight to bring Weebit along. He smiled, hopeful they had found their new home already. Sighing his relief, he got to his feet and gazed at the stately tree that stood over the cave, one last enjoyable moment before he went back to work. A dim glow of light showed him where the entrance was and he mused at how peaceful the woods were. He sighed again as an extra loud swearword interrupted the night.

CHAPTER TWO

Clever glanced around the cave from where he stood near the entrance and decided it looked as if an explosive device had gone off. But if he ignored the clutter of wood shavings and piles of dirt, there was now a table and temporary seats in the centre, the beginnings of a cooking pit, and four sleeping pads up against the far wall. Weebit was standing in the middle of the cave, wearing a calculating expression, while the others were seated at the new beautifully carved table. Clever walked over and joined them.

"Okay," said Sarge, "this will do for base camp. Let's get out there and check it out."

Clever grumbled under his breath and tried to wrestle back the leadership. "Sterling notion," he said. "Those configurations of trees need further examination, and we really must confirm the proximity of the nearest humans."

"Whut?"

"I *said*, 'good idea', Nimin."

"Oh."

They watched Weebit assessing the cave until he felt their eyes on him and glanced over. Sarge raised an eyebrow and Weebit nodded, satisfied. Clever narrowed his eyes at Sarge's back. Walnut.

The group stopped behind a tree at the outside of the woods and used its roots as a shield to peer around at the scenery before them. Out of the protective shadows of the woods, the area appeared as idyllic as it had the night before. The distant pond sparkled silvery-blue, the grass still in shadow shone with moisture, and it was so still and quiet that Clever could hear a bee buzzing from two trees away. A small black shadow passed across the middle of the grass and he squinted up to watch a bird gliding well above the ground. He turned his head to signal to the others and they moved off, Sarge nodding approval and Nimin and Weebit smiling broadly, as they all stepped out from the smell of pine needles and earth to stand in the bright sunshine.

They walked in the other direction from the pond, skirting along the side of the woods, before veering across an open expanse of grass towards one of the rows of trees on the other side. Once they reached the row, Clever paused between two of the trees to purse his lips and consider the uniform line stretching out to both sides.

"You can study your trees later, Clever," said an impatient Sarge, not slowing his pace, but instead marching between the trees and striding out onto the next field of grass. Clever glared after him, just as Sarge suddenly stumbled and disappeared. Clever only just beat the others to where Sarge had fallen, and stopped at the edge of what turned out to be an enormous hole in the ground. They watched as Sarge rolled, head tucked in and arms and legs flailing, right down to the bottom of the empty pond. He did one last massive flip and a final slide before landing face-up at the bottom, completely still and half covered with sand.

"Sarge? Are you okay, Sarge?" called Nimin, his voice rising with panic.

Sarge replied through gritted teeth, "I'm

just resting. It's such a lovely spot down here, why don't you join me?"

"Oh, okay then." Nimin was stepping over the edge when Clever grabbed his arm.

"Sarcasm, Nimin. You really must learn to understand the concept of sarcasm."

#

Once Sarge had climbed out from the sandy pit and dusted himself off – the set of his jaw convincing Clever not to say a word – the group had continued on their way across the grass.

Eventually, several rows of trees since leaving the woods, they popped out near the far end of a field from the building.

"There are humans over there," nodded Sarge, indicating a red brick building with big windows and large writing over the wide doorway.

"Restaurantandbar" read Clever, screwing up his face to squint at the distant letters. "That's unusual. They don't typically place a name on their houses." He took a minute to consider the brick building. "Still, it's sufficiently yonder not to interfere with our activities, I propose," he continued.

Nimin looked at Sarge for an explanation.

"He means they won't bother us."

"This locality appears to be acceptable, I believe," said Clever, with a furrowed brow. When Sarge nodded his agreement, Nimin grinned, clapping his hands together and obviously thrilled they had said 'yes' to the place with the fishes pond and pretty grounds. They turned around to head back to the woods when there was a small noise from behind them, coming from the direction of the distant building. *Toc*! Clever spun around first and scowled towards the building. Then he looked up, his eyes boggling.

"Incoming!" he yelled.

The Dinglemen scattered as a fast-moving white missile landed amongst them.

Donk!

It ricocheted off the ground, bounced twice and dribbled to a stop several metres away. Clever and Sarge walked across to check it out, both prodding at the round projectile and muttering. Clever was so intrigued by the missile he hardly noticed when Nimin and Weebit finally ventured out from under nearby shrubbery, although they still kept their distance and looked ready to bolt.

"Must have failed to go off," said Sarge, giving it a hard enough prod for the missile to roll.

"Gracious! Be careful!"

"Why? It's obviously a dud."

"I, for one, don't want it going off in my face, that's why." Clever pulled his eyes away from the missile to look back at the building, a confused look on his face.

"They've never attacked us before, and besides, how would they know we're here?"

"I don't care," said Sarge, glaring towards the building. "Those humans are trying to start a war. I *like* it here and we don't have—"

He broke off and gaped at the scene in the distance, where several humans were lining up with what appeared to be sticks in their hands. Sarge and Clever both squinted to see what they were doing, while a rapid pounding behind them turned out to be Nimin, racing for cover at the far end of the field. Weebit's guileless eyes questioned Clever and Sarge, and then he looked over his shoulder to where Nimin was weaving towards the trees. Visibly deciding Nimin was displaying more intelligence, he turned and raced after him, overtaking him just as they reached the safety of the stand of trees.

Donk! Donk!

With missiles raining down around them, Clever and Sarge glanced at each other in horror, spun around and raced towards Nimin's wildly waving arms.

Donk! Donk!

They all stared from the undergrowth as more of the missiles flew across the ground, thudded into the turf, bounced and rolled.

"Rotten shots, aren't they?" commented Sarge.

Fascinated, Clever and Sarge watched as the white missiles collected in the area, not one of them exploding. Every single one a dud! What atrocious workmanship, thought Clever. Even so, a white-faced Nimin tried to sidle away from the scene until Sarge snagged his collar and held him firmly with a clenched fist. He hadn't removed his eyes from the gathering missiles. Clever noticed Weebit was looking up into the greenery behind them. He had lost interest in the missiles already and was probably, Clever thought, looking to see if the branches held any parrots.

"You know, Sarge, it is indicated that these

missiles have absolutely nothing to do with us," said Clever, his gaze back on the covered ground ahead, and impressed with himself for keeping up the academic leader speak under fire.

Sarge wasn't convinced, "Hmmm."

The barrage stopped. The missiles blanketed the area where they had been standing, and some had almost rolled all the way to where they were sheltering in the trees. Sarge glared at Nimin, who was now hopping from foot to foot. Nimin stopped his wriggling but still looked as if he desperately wanted to be somewhere else. He pointed a trembling finger towards the building in the distance.

A human was walking towards them. It was pulling along a little white cart and it looked as if it was speaking, which seemed a bit odd because the human was alone.

"Be silent," Sarge hissed at Nimin, who didn't need telling twice. He was staring round-eyed at the approaching human and was completely dumbstruck.

"Be my girl, woo woh, heey—," sang the human as it came within earshot, although with no discernible tune and sounding awful.

The human started to collect the white missiles and put them into the cart, bopping in time to a beat only it could hear.

Clever watched with increasingly gleaming eyes. He was starting to realise the full potential of his studies if Dingledell was moved here. First, he would find out what the white missiles were for and why the trees were in rows, and then, with the humans living so near, he would be able to design and conduct long-term research on his subjects. He could learn so much more about their daily interactions. Perhaps even study an entire family unit? Feeling suddenly giddy, his eyes widened at the possibilities. The amount of data he would be able to collect would surely push his research far beyond what he had ever managed before. Especially as a lot of his current knowledge was gleaned from reading their discarded papers. Just imagine, he mused, if he didn't have to rely on their wasteful way with words.

Clever began to make mental notes about the specimen ahead of them, concentrating so hard he forgot the others were standing beside him. This was a young one, maybe thirteen or fourteen years old. It appeared to be of average height for its age, and slim, as if it never quite got enough to eat. It had brown floppy hair that fell into large brown eyes. Clever noted the other facial features as unremarkable. Not too big, not too small, not crooked, no outstanding markings. The human also had that disjointed look the young males often seemed to have, with knobbly knees and the legs too long for its body. Its wiggling and bopping to the silent music highlighted awkward hip motion. How he wished he could speak to it! He could achieve so much by talking to a human, and this one really appeared completely harmless. He wondered – if he trapped it, maybe—

"Be my baaaby—"

"I might have to gag it," he muttered under his breath.

#

Clever could hear Weebit humming and he looked pleased with himself, which Clever took as a good omen. Weebit was scanning the cave with a critical eye, and Clever knew he was picturing where the tunnels would begin and where chambers would be built off the main cavern. His focused stance reminded Clever of when Weebit had extended an area in his laboratory for his growing collection of human paraphernalia. Weebit had created the perfect space for the collection, and Clever had finally been able to bring home and label as many items as he could carry from his research trips. As he had done then, Weebit was absently stroking his favourite axe handle as he calculated tunnel heights and lengths and the placement of chambers. It was riveting to watch as Weebit's eyes travelled slowly around the cave, mentally placing steps here, an entrance there, his gaze slowly rising up through the wood of the tree trunk above them. Weebit had a fascination with lookouts and had placed many throughout the upper reaches of Dingledell. Shaking his head, Clever corrected himself – the *previous* Dingledell. He had once overheard one of the elders telling Weebit that, in fact, you could have too many lookouts. Clever wondered how many Weebit would get away with during the building of an entire Dingledell and not just the expansion of an existing one. No wonder he looked so pleased with himself.

#

Peter was singing again. It was the first afternoon of his summer holidays and he had two whole months of freedom ahead of him. Well, working at the club, but that was better than being stuck in a classroom to his way of thinking. His afternoon job was to find the golf balls that had been lost in the rough grass along the fairways. Any balls that he found around the course were returned to the club and sold back to golfers so they could lose them again. Given that the majority of the Breadalbone club members were rotten at the game, there were plenty of lost balls to be found. Wandering along in the sunshine bathing the side of fairway eighteen, he grimaced as a thought struck him. He would have to get the golf balls out of the pond again this summer. Last year, he had stepped on a carp. It shot out from under him, but he could still remember the feel of slimy skin against his foot. Erghh. He shuddered at the memory. Just then, he thought he saw the tint of a fluro-yellow golf ball in the long grass ahead of him. He pounced.

\#

Clever wondered what the young human was doing right now. He could see Sarge was getting impatient waiting for Weebit to sort himself out, and he could sympathise. Really, Weebit might be a genius, but just how long does genius need to put a tunnel into a wall? Sarge snorted with satisfaction when Weebit finally looked at him and nodded towards where he wanted him to start work. Clever knew he wouldn't be needed for a while and idly considered heading over to check out what the humans were doing. He was curious to know what the brick building was used for, and the dud missiles were really bugging him. Why launch them, then go out and pick them up again? It just didn't make sense, but he was sure if he could observe long enough he would be able to determine the answer. Sarge sauntered over to where Weebit indicated and swung his pick at the cave wall. Clever was still thinking of the human as he watched Sarge powering through the earth, with tree roots, dirt and wood chips flying out behind him.

#

Peter had worked his way through the long grass and under the trees flanking the fairway of number seventeen. Only another sixteen fairways to go, and then he could start all over again. He wondered why the worst of the golfers didn't take the hint of golf ball expense and take up another sport. He put his basket down and straightened as a golf cart zoomed up, the dour groundskeeper passed over a wrapped package of food and a bottle of water, grunted something under his breath, and spun the cart back the way it had come. Peter smiled his thanks at the groundskeeper's back. The package contained a couple of doughnuts, smelling of sweet warmth, covered in icing sugar and oozing with fresh cream and strawberry jam. He suddenly realised why the golfers were prepared to put up with constantly losing golf balls and, periodically, their temper – the food.

#

Clever glanced across the table at Nimin, who was swinging his legs and watching Sarge powering through the wall, a slightly dopey expression on his face and his head nodding in time with Sarge's pick. Weebit was staring at Sarge's back, too, making sure the tunnel was exactly where and how he wanted it. Nimin looked happy enough to sit and watch, but Clever was becoming bored. He heard a loud grunt from Sarge and a pile of wood chips spewed out of the tunnel mouth. One of the larger wood chips flew across the cavern and whistled past his ear, making up his mind for him. It would be safer outside.

Fairway sixteen had only given up three balls. Peter stepped onto fairway fifteen and squinted at the woods that lined the back of the golf course. He had discovered just how big they were last summer, by spending hours roving about in there without finding enough golf balls to make it worth the effort. So now, he only went in as far as the first few metres and didn't attempt to wander in much farther.

#

Clever went outside. He had planned to go across to the brick building but had discovered humans passing right by the woods. They were walloping the dud missiles with shiny metal sticks, walking up to where they landed, and smacking them again. He was thrilled to see the humans came right to him. He would be able to sit *right here* and work out why they would want to hit defenseless little missiles around. Moving Dingledell to this new place was going to make his research so much easier. No more long expeditions, no more detailed preparation, no more hiking for hours and hours. Clever sighed happily, and it was just then that he spied the young human with the knobbly knees, moving along under the trees and heading right towards where he stood.

#

Peter was concentrating on the pine needles ahead, scouring the ground for half-hidden golf balls while attempting to avoid tripping on tree roots. Suddenly, the hairs on the back of his neck stood straight up and he felt just like a bug under a microscope.

CHAPTER THREE

Peter looked up to see a tiny man, all of about seven centimetres high, standing on the pine needles a few metres ahead of him. He supposed the excited-looking apparition was a trick of his imagination and thought that maybe he should get more sleep. He closed his eyes, knuckled his sockets and rubbed his eyelids to clear his vision, and then glanced at the ground again. The tiny figure was still there. Peter wondered if it was a hologram, but for all his tiny size the man seemed, well, solid. And why would there be a hologram in some woods at the back of a golf course in Breadalbone, of all places? The little man didn't move or speak but kept watching him with such an intense stare that Peter got the feeling he was expected to say something.

"Um, hello?" said Peter.

Less than twenty minutes later, Peter was

sitting against the base of a tree and the little man was comfortably perched on his knee. The man's small features were sharp, with a long nose that quivered as he waved his hands about in effusive explanation of his interest in humans. He had introduced himself as Clever and had said he was a scientist. Peter's mind was still struggling with having a man small enough to be preening on his knee without thinking about his profession. And the man *was* preening. He was smoothing down his white shirt and giving the impression of being well-groomed and well aware of it. Peter wondered if he was an elf and looked for pointed ears. He discovered that, if anything, the man's ears were more rounded than his own, half-hidden by a shock of dark hair. Peter couldn't remember what else he had read about elves, but he was pretty sure they had pointed ears. And weren't real, a voice in his head reminded him. And besides, would elves ask so many questions? Maybe the man was a pixie. And what shaped ears did pixies have?

"And something else I would like to know, why do you humans eat sparrow-grass?"

"Sparrow-grass? You mean asparagus?

Search me."

"Really? May I? What would I find?"

The little man, Clever, listened intently to him, eyes shining and head nodding as Peter tried to answer his questions. When Peter finally managed to ask a question himself, Clever told him he was a Dingleman, and that humans didn't ever see them, partly because humans only see half of what is actually there, but mostly because they avoided being seen.

"But – I'm seeing you," Peter said.

The delight on Clever's face faded as he apparently realised the enormity of what he had done. He had *shown* himself to a human. He turned pale and scrambled down from Peter's knee, backing away hurriedly from his shoe. Peter only just managed to put his hand behind him to stop him from leaving, engulfing him within his palm.

"Please. Don't go. I won't hurt you. And I won't say anything!"

Clever's eyes widened, but he stopped backing away.

"I promise, I won't say anything to anyone. Who'd believe me anyway? And I can tell you anything you want to know about people, I don't mind."

It only took a moment longer to convince Clever. Just as he looked to be seriously considering Peter's offer for information, the bush across from them exploded in a flurry of rage and three more of the little men galloped at him, waving their weapons and screaming.

"*ARRGGHHH!*"

Peter yelped and tried to shift his feet out of the way, but they moved too fast. The largest of them brought down his pick in a wide, blurred arc and stabbed Peter in the big toe.

"Yeoww!"

Peter grabbed his foot and rocked, while Clever yelled at the biggest one to stop. He didn't need to yell at the other two. Both had halted well away from Peter, where they goggled at him from a safe distance. Through tears of pain, he saw a chubby Dingleman trying to hide behind a tiny man with wild red hair. The red-haired Dingleman seemed unfocused, more interested in the axe he held than in the human rocking in agony in front of him. Clever yelled at the bigger Dingleman again, but he kept his weapon held high, turned a furious red and yelled back in a torrent of swearwords and pick-waving. Peter scrunched back against the bark of the tree behind him, tucking his feet as far away from the waving pick as possible.

"It's all right, Sarge!" said Clever. "I've been conversing with him for the last twenty minutes. The human's name is Peter and he's friendly."

"It is not *all right*," raged the one called Sarge. "It's a human and it's seen us and now—"

He broke off and turned on Clever.

"Did I just hear you say that you've been *talking* to it? Are you *insane*?"

Peter warily eyed the one called Sarge, fascinated by what could only be called a tiny whirlwind of terrible rage. Sarge was still ranting at Clever when the little red-haired man's eyes finally settled on Peter and his head cocked to one side. Peter felt himself summed up in seconds and judged to be harmless. The man put down his axe, bowed in a dignified manner, and nodded at him.

"Weebit," was all he said.

It was enough to shock the one called Sarge into silence. The chubby Dingleman had backed up a few paces when Weebit put his axe down and now just looked prepared to run away.

"N-Nimin," he squeaked.

Sarge looked thunderous, the pick still quivering enough for Peter to keep an eye on the sharp edge, his hands covering his feet just in case Sarge decided he hadn't finished spearing toes. Peter tried to smile, but it felt as if it came out more as a grimace.

"Um, hi? I'm Peter."

"What sort of name is Peter?" asked Sarge rudely.

"Ooh, good question," said Clever. He turned back to Peter and raised an expressive eyebrow, leaning forward for the answer.

"Er, just a name, I guess. My parents gave it to me. I didn't choose it."

"Does it have a meaning?" asked Clever, suddenly looking as if he could happily resume his interrogation from earlier. Weebit and Nimin inched forward to stand behind the comparative bulk of Sarge.

"Its actual meaning is, um, a stone or rock, I think."

"A stone? Like a grey, over-sized pebble? That sort of stone?" asked Clever, with a confused frown.

"That's weird," whispered the one called

Nimin to Sarge.

"It's not weird. It's stupid," declared Sarge, loudly.

"Absolutely fascinating," mused Clever. "It would appear humans don't obtain their nomenclature in the same manner as ourselves."

"What?" said Nimin, glancing at Sarge. Sarge looked as if he was sulking and just shook his head. He lowered his pick, but swung it gently at his feet while staring at Peter, a belligerent expression on his face.

"I mean, they don't get named in the same way that we do."

"Oh."

Peter was interested. "How are you named?"

"We're given our names as our calling becomes clear," Clever explained. He thrust out his chest and raised his chin. "I was named at a very young age, as my superior intelligence was noticeable during even the earliest phases of growth."

Peter could see that Sarge was muttering sourly while making faces at the back of Clever's head. Peter assumed the others had heard this boast once or twice before.

"So it's a bit like nicknames?"

"No, no, we earn them, we don't steal them," said Clever, shaking his head. "For example, Sarge earned his name because he's strong and tough."

Sarge's smile was thin.

"He's a warrior," said Clever. Sarge nodded.

"Brave." A nod.

"Resolute." Another nod.

"Bossy."

"Bossy? I'm not bossy! Nimin, tell the human I'm not bossy," said Sarge, glaring at Clever and then at Peter.

"What about the others?" asked Peter quickly, pursing his lips to stop a smile. He didn't want to risk losing another toenail.

"Nimin is our cook."

"Nimin?'

"Yeah, you know. Nimin. Lambchops." Nimin had forgotten to be scared of Peter and walked closer as he nodded agreement.

"Um, okay. And Weebit?"

"Oh, well, he's a wee bit with us, but not exactly, completely, *with* us," said Clever.

"He's our architect," piped up Nimin.

"He functions extremely well when designing, creating or building, but doesn't really think about anything else, apart from-"

"He's a loopy," said Sarge.

"Apart from when he is in the company of femmes. He has a talent for understanding them, too." Clever frowned, as if this talent was a much harder ability to fathom than Weebit's being a master architect.

"Femmes? You mean girls, females?" asked Peter.

"Yes, indeed, he has a gift."

Peter blinked, wondering how many of these tiny men were living within the woods. He risked a brief glance around just in case he was now surrounded by thousands of them, all carrying picks and as grumpy as Sarge. He could only see the four he had been talking to.

"And where are they? The females?"

"Oh, they aren't anywhere near here," said Clever evasively.

"But we'll be bringing—mmnfffft." Nimin was cut off by Sarge's hand clamped over his mouth.

"We really must be getting back now," said Clever quickly, backing away. "It's been nice to talk to you, though. Must be getting on, bye bye."

Nimin was dragged backward on his heels

by Sarge, a hand still clamped over his mouth. Weebit stood still with unblinking eyes trained on Peter, and then he finally seemed to notice the others' retreat and trailed off in their wake.

"Wait! Can I meet with you again?"

The Dinglemen glanced at each other, with Sarge glaring at Clever, and then they all leaned into a tight huddle. Clever was nodding and gesturing as he spoke, and Peter could hear snippets of speech, "useful – harmless – can't – research." Nimin was nodding along, but Sarge was shaking his head vigorously, obviously horrified that Clever was even contemplating the idea. Clever turned to Peter.

"As group leader and spokesperson, I would like to say that we accept your proposal."

Sarge's scowl was bigger than he was.

#

Peter was glad it was the end of the work-day because he didn't have a hope of concentrating on collecting golf balls. He walked back towards the clubrooms, thinking about the Dinglemen and wondering if he had fallen asleep against the tree and dreamed of them. He was determined to keep them to himself, even if people would believe him, which he knew they wouldn't. If he started claiming sightings of tiny little men he would be put into a hospital in a white padded cell and be wrapped up in a straight-jacket.

He was so deep in thought he strode into a bunker and walked straight across the middle instead of bothering to walk around. Kicking up sand, he wondered how long it had been since a human had talked with the Dinglemen or maybe even been their friend. He had the feeling he would have to work hard to impress Sarge.

As soon as Peter finished work the next day, he visited the woods behind fairway fifteen to see if the Dinglemen were really there. He whistled as he walked along the trees to alert them that he was visiting and crossed his fingers that they would respond. He had brought them some of his mother's baking as a gift, aptly named rock cakes, in which even the sultanas were like granite. His father had raised his eyebrows when Peter had helped himself to a couple and stashed them in a pocket.

A tiny body popped around the bottom of one of the tree trunks and Clever waved him over. Surprisingly, the others were all there with him, although Sarge stood with his arms crossed and looked pained to see him again. Peter made sure he was out of sight of any passing golfers and sat down to offer the rock cakes, apologising that they might be a bit hard. Nimin pounced on the offering, opened his jaws wide, and with a lot of lip smacking and loud chomping, gobbled a path through the middle of one of the cakes, tiny waves of crumbs spurting out as he ate. Peter couldn't help but stare to see if Nimin would plough right through until he stumbled out the other side. He heard a shout from people on the fairway and leaned sideways to get a look.

"What are they doing?" asked Clever.

"They're playing golf," said Peter. He briefly told them about the game and answered their questions, mostly from Clever who was fascinated that so much effort went into a pursuit that didn't appear to have much point.

"So, Clever, how come you didn't know about this golf?" asked Sarge.

"Well, I—it must be new. Is it new, Peter?"

"Um—"

"There you go. I can't be expected to know about new things. Anyway, Peter, you were saying this area is specially designed for people to chase their little balls around?"

"Well, if you put it like that, yeah, I guess so," said Peter.

"That is stupid," declared Sarge.

"And it's very important to humans, this area?"

"I'd say so, yes."

"This golf isn't just a phase?"

"No. No, it's not a phase. The golf course will probably be here for a very long time."

"Really, human? And how do you know that? If this golf is so new?" asked Sarge.

"Well, um, actually, it's been around for centuries."

Clever turned pink and glared at a smirking Sarge. He muttered something that was drowned out by a loud burp from Nimin.

"You know, you could live here in the woods," said Peter, sure that Clever wanted to make this area their home and maybe even bring others here to live.

"People don't build over golf courses. And nobody walks very far into the trees looking for lost balls. And the woods are huge. They've always belonged to the golf club, I think." He suddenly knew he really wanted the Dinglemen to stay. "And did I mention the river? There's a river on the other side of the woods, so the only access is from the golf course."

Clever looked pleased, and Nimin and Weebit, both now seated on a nearby tree root, smiled happily. Looking at Sarge's cloudy expression, however, Peter couldn't help feeling worried that Sarge would convince them all to leave. Peter had a brilliant idea of how he could show the Dinglemen the layout of the golf course and the size of the woods from the air, but looking at the small faces in front of him he thought it best to leave it until later to make his suggestion. Saying his goodbyes, he left the Dinglemen for the night, with Nimin insisting on rolling the remaining rock cake back to their new home for a snack for later. Peter had walked several metres away, and was wondering how long they had been living in the woods and where they had come from, when he felt a piercing jab in the side of his foot.

"Ow!" Peter rubbed his foot through his sneaker and looked down into the blazing eyes of Sarge.

"Don't give me that! I didn't kick you hard. I just want your undivided attention." Sarge folded his arms and kept up the glare. "Let's get something straight, human. I don't trust you and I don't like you. And I don't like it that Clever likes you, even if it is just as a test subject. You might have the others fooled, but not me. Don't go thinking you're our friend. Understand? I'm watching you."

He didn't wait for Peter to reply. He just turned and left, disappearing back into the undergrowth.

CHAPTER FOUR

As soon as he had forced down a morning meal Clever went outside. He was deliberately avoiding Sarge but knew he wouldn't be able to keep it up for much longer. For several days, he had managed to stay out of Sarge's way by spending time out in the woods, informing the others he was inspecting the surrounding area, but really he was just dodging another confrontation. He thought of the meetings they'd had with Peter and smiled. Then he remembered the arguments he'd had with Sarge and his smile faded.

He briefly wondered what the elders were thinking when they choose him for the mission. Then he wondered what *he* was thinking when he chose Sarge to accompany him.

At least it was a warm sunny day, perfect

for human watching, so he decided to head over to see what might be happening at the golf house. There was no harm in doing some research while he was out and about, he thought, as he sped between trees and across the green grassways. Finally pausing under the shrubs at the front of the building, Clever decided he had an acceptable view of several humans lounging around the outside tables. The tables, with their green sun umbrellas, were arranged to give easy access to the building through wide open doors while offering the best views of the grounds.

He heard a *'swish, toc'* just behind him and turned to watch a golf player stare after his ball and then swagger to his large bag of bobble-headed sticks. Clever watched as a group of four humans took turns to hit their balls away and then stroll off down the length of grass to chase after them, still wondering why they would go to all that effort just to end up back at the start, as Peter had explained.

He turned his attention back to the humans at the tables, listening to the babble of voices and faint clattering of cutlery against plates. Shifting closer to the nearest table, he skulked under the shrubs rimming the balconied area until he was almost directly underneath where three middle-aged females were drinking out of dainty porcelain cups and scoffing down a small mountain of frosted cakes.

Just then, he spied a young female exit the wide doorway from the building, cross the balcony and trot down the stairs. She carried an empty black bag over a shoulder and he was curious to know what she was going to put into it. Sidling past the last of the shrubs, he saw the female walking along the line of trees bordering the grassway nearest the end of the building. With a spurt of speed he crossed to the trees, his eyes trained on the back of his quarry. Clever recognised the grassway as the one they had been standing on when they first observed the golf house. Remembering the white balls raining down around him he couldn't help himself, he instinctively looked back towards the building to check for assailants.

He trotted to catch up with the female, who was rapidly moving away, stopping once to pick something up and stash it in the bag. He crept closer, hearing her mutter to herself as she scanned the undergrowth for whatever it was that she was hunting. Clever estimated that she was about Peter's age, although she was much smaller than Peter, her clothes hanging off a petite frame. She had pale hair, cut to her chin and a small turned-up nose. He got as close as he could, watched her pick up a drinking can, drop it into the bag and move on.

"Pigs, the lot of them," she said aloud.

Clever wondered if he was going to gain any valuable information following her around to collect discarded materials and considered heading back to the golf house, but decided to follow the young female a little longer. She led him into the stand of trees where he and the others had sheltered from the barrage of golf missiles, then she cut off to the right, bent to pick something up, wound her way between the trees and popped out into a small clearing. Clever stopped under a shrub at the edge of the clearing, just in time to hear a giggle and watch a glass bottle fly through the air and land close to where he and the female were standing.

"HEY!"

Clever peered between her ankles to see who she was yelling at. Two humans, a male and a female, were sitting close together on a spread blanket, a cane basket sitting behind them and a small banquet of sandwiches, cheeses, fruit and cakes spread out on plates around them. They didn't turn their heads to look across at the female and they didn't appear to have heard her. Each held up a glass filled with a pale gold liquid and gently tapped it against the glass held by the other. They smiled and sipped. The male put down his glass, shifted position to reach into a pocket in his shorts and pulled out a tiny container, flipping the lid to show his companion what was inside. His eyes never left her face.

"I *said*, Hey!"

Clever glanced around the small clearing. It was really very pleasant, cool and shady, with soft mossy grass and an air of privacy. The two humans looked over, surprised that the female was standing there and yelling at them.

"Daisy! Do you mind?" asked the male, with a pained look on his face.

"Well, now that you ask me, yes! Yes, I do mind," said the glowering Daisy. She stalked to where the green bottle had landed, plucked it off the ground and brandished it at the couple. Clever noticed the female on the blanket couldn't keep her eyes off the little box, despite his research subject, Daisy, posturing and barking, waving the bottle as she lectured and pointed at them with a reproachful finger. She reminded Clever of Sarge. He listened while she told them off for their littering and their total lack of respect for the land they lived on, land that provided them with clothing and housing and gave them apple trees. He listened while she growled and ranted and flayed them for their atrocious behaviour.

"I'm trying to propose here!"

"Oh."

That seemed to stop her, momentarily. She looked thoughtful as the female on the blanket threw her arms around the male's neck and kissed him, only pulling away to beam some more at the little box.

"Tony, of course I'll marry you!"

A human bonding offer! He scratched his memory for the name. An engagement? Clever was thrilled. He couldn't believe how lucky he was to be present at such a ceremonious event.

"Are you sure you want to marry him?" asked Daisy. "It seems to me, he's a bit of a slob."

"I would have picked it up. C'mon, Daisy, we want to celebrate." The male glared at her. "Could we please have some privacy here? Please? Pretty please?"

"Hmm, well, all right, but I'll be checking the area once you're gone. And just remember, I know where to find you to torture you."

"No kidding," the male muttered.

Daisy nodded curtly at them and turned back towards the way she had come. Clever looked at the pair huddled together on the blanket, a dopey smile spreading across his face. He was torn between staying and watching the couple or following his current subject. She had led him to see the bonding offer. Where else might she be heading, and what would he miss if he stayed here? He cast a final wistful glance over his shoulder and chased after Daisy. Weaving between the trees behind her, and keeping an eye on the flashes of blue fabric and black bag just ahead of him, he thought about what he had just witnessed. He was a bit disappointed to admit that, as an occasion, he had really thought a human bonding offer would be more, well, romantic.

#

Later that day, Clever glanced around at the work already completed within the cave and wasn't quite able to decide how he felt. He knew this place was perfect for them. It was a logical choice, and besides, he could just feel it was right, which he admitted to himself might not be the most scientific approach to making a decision. Still, it was within a big area of woods, it was inside the human city, bounded by a river and the protected grassways. It was exactly what the elders had asked him to find. And the cavern under the tree had the potential to be just as good as the old Dingledell and that wasn't something at which to snort. Now that he thought about it some more, if they chose to stay here, he would soon be known as the one who delivered the new Dingledell. He smirked at the idea, dreaming of being seated within an admiring group of femmes, a rich ruby-coloured cape draped around his shoulders and dishes of chopped berries and nuts, and perhaps even a strawberry, within easy reach. Well, all right, he thought, when figs fly, but it would be nice. His eyes roamed around the primary living cavern under the tree, taking in some of the intricate detail already carved into the walls, the half-finished tunnels still somehow giving the impression of devoted artistry and craftsmanship. Weebit was racing ahead with designing and creating their new home. If only Sarge wasn't such a prejudiced, belligerent, irritating, not-to-mention stubborn, opinionated, sardonic, squiggle-eyed...ignorant bogging drongle. He couldn't think of any more disparaging words.

"I've been looking for you," said Sarge from behind him.

Clever sighed. Just his luck, he thought.

"Have you?"

"Yes. Stand still, so I can talk to you."

Clever didn't trust his voice not to squeak, so he just raised an eyebrow as Sarge squared up to him and stayed quiet. Sarge mistook this for arrogance and glared at him.

"I don't like this place. I don't like Peter. I think you are insane for getting us involved with a *human*." He spat the word, warmed to his tirade and wound up towards a bellow.

"I can't believe you'd trust him! How can you trust a human? I don't care how stupid you think he is, it'll only lead to trouble."

Sarge loomed forward as he yelled. "What do you think you're doing? Are you prepared to fail the elders, fail all of us, just so you can conduct your *research*? And just what do you think they are going to say about us getting tangled up with a bogging human?"

Clever felt a wall at his back and was surprised to realise he had been moving backward while Sarge sprayed spittle at him as he ranted. He wiped at his cheek with a finger, enraging Sarge even more.

"How can you even *think* about bringing everyone here! It's not safe with a human knowing we're here. I can't believe you could be so stupid! The elders have made a huge mistake choosing *you* for this job."

Clever was glad to know that Nimin and Weebit were out getting their dinner. He would be mortified if they were present for this. If he was the type to keep score, so far Sarge was ahead by at least fifteen to nothing. He twisted his hands behind his back and cleared his throat.

"Oh, you feel like saying something now, huh?" said Sarge. "Well, thank you very much, sir, leader, sir! Do you need a few minutes to think of some big words?"

Clever had finally had enough. He held up a hand. "This location is acceptable. In fact, this is just what we were asked to find." He was glad his voice came out normally and he didn't think Sarge could detect he was shaking.

"The location would be better if you hadn't gone inviting the local wildlife to visit us when it felt like it!"

"Peter is going to be a great help to us, and yes, I do trust him! Weebit and Nimin love this place for our new home, and they like and trust Peter, too. It's more private here than any other park we'll find within a human city. Did you think we'd move to a city and not have them all around us? This is the best place for us! You'll see."

"This location isn't secure. Even if we don't include all of the humans you'd like to invite to live with us, there are still predators out there. It's not safe here, Clever, so don't go pretending you're any sort of success just yet!"

Clever narrowed his eyes and raised his voice. "If I recall correctly, Sarge, securing the area is *your* job!"

Sarge spluttered with rage. "What's the point when you're working against me? How many humans will be coming to dine with us this evening, hmm?"

"Only Peter." Clever couldn't help an evil grin.

Sarge was momentarily speechless. He obviously hadn't been expecting Clever to grin at him. Clever had not expected it himself. He took advantage of Sarge's loss of words to escape, hearing a frustrated hiss behind him. He walked away with a stiff back and his head held high until he thought he was far enough away from the entrance under the tree that he could let himself relax.

He slumped against a tree root and let out his breath. He didn't think Sarge had followed, and he was grateful for getting away without having Sarge stalking along behind to continue the assault. Clever didn't know what he was going do to get Sarge to see how good they had it here. He did know that it was going to take a miracle.

#

Peter was talking to the statue of Captain Breadalbone while he scrubbed bird droppings off the shoulders. The statue was a centrepiece in one of the gardens, and Captain Breadalbone a forefather of the city and someone who was, apparently, a bit eccentric. Peter remembered learning that he had lived on a large black yacht, perched high and dry on the land he had eventually given to the city for the golf course. The Captain had liked boats but hated water. Peter thought he was someone who would have appreciated the Dinglemen. He would have believed in them. Peter imagined the Captain would have invited them to live within the hull of his black ship, where they could live in safety and comfort in return for keeping him amused. Not that they would have accepted, Peter thought quickly, feeling guilty that his musings almost had them sounding like pets.

It was a warm day for hard scrubbing – overcast, with pale grey, fluffy clouds. He had also discovered that he had to be super careful because the ladder wobbled on the gravel of the driveway, forcing him to keep a grip on the statue as he worked. The concrete making up the shoulders of the Captain's jacket was moulded into tasselled epaulets and it was making getting the bird poop off more trouble than he had thought. He was beginning to think the birds aimed for the deep crevasses between the tassels just to make his life more difficult. He used to find it amusing to see birds perched on the Captain's shoulders, and with the statue's eye patch, pipe and captain's uniform, a bird ruffling its feathers on the shoulder fitted the picture perfectly. He had found it amusing, that is, until he found out that cleaning the statue was *his* job.

Clever had resumed his investigations of the grounds and was still making himself scarce from their new Dingledell. During the morning, Nimin and Weebit had stared at the granite expression on Sarge's face, worriedly glanced at Clever, looked again at Sarge, and then turned questioning eyes back onto Clever. He finally couldn't handle the pressure and had escaped to conduct some more research. Telling the others he was doing some scouting of the area, checking for potential dangers, he had made his escape. Sarge hadn't commented but his mouth had twitched.

It felt so good to be out and about, and away from Sarge's scorn, that Clever decided to explore well away from Dingledell. He paced across the grassways between the woods and scooted to the black fence that ran adjacent to the other side of the golf house. The fence led him right along to where there was a large tended grass area, gardens, a pebbled road, and an area for parking motorcars. This is where he came across Peter, perched on top of a ladder and cleaning a tall stone model of a human. Clever maneuvered himself closer, moving in from the fence to a garden bed situated between the grass and the edge of the pebbled road. He sighed and relaxed, sitting down on a dark fragrant woodchip under a plant with yellow-petalled flowers, from where he could peer up and observe.

Peter appeared lost in thought and Clever wondered what he was thinking about. He had watched him enough in the last few days to know that Peter could show a range of expressions while conducting the same job, but often he just looked as if he was thinking of something else. Clever smiled and wiggled to get comfortable. He enjoyed nothing more than Peter-watching. Predicting his behaviour, analysing his expressions, dissecting his actions – all of this was becoming Clever's idea of quality entertainment. Just for a little while, he would be able to forget about Dingledell and Sarge, and shuck all of the responsibility off his shoulders. He would be able to forget all about the elders and their expectations. He would be able to–

"Clever! Wohoo? Hey, Clever?"

Clever spun around to see Nimin barrelling through the grass, bouncing off the black fence in wild excitement.

"Over here!" he hissed.

He saw Sarge tear up behind Nimin, his expression even stormier than usual, and then Weebit trailing through the grass well behind Sarge. Clever leapt to his feet. What was going on? Nimin careened into him as he raced into the woodchips and gabbled out his news.

"I found mushrooms! Wild ones, in the woods. So they're just for us!" He bounced on his toetips, eyes spinning in his head. "I loovve mushrooms!"

Clever glanced towards Peter, but it didn't look as if he had heard a thing. Sarge skidded into the garden.

"Didn't you hear me, you inkblot? What were you thinking? There's a predator out there! I told you to stop!"

"What?" said Clever.

"You heard me," snapped Sarge. "I sighted it after you left," he said, turning back to Nimin to tell him off some more.

"You couldn't wait for Clever to come back to tell him, could you? You just couldn't wait? You are not to go running off until I've eliminated the danger, do you understand me?"

"Sarge," said Clever.

"Why don't you ever think?"

"Sarge!"

"I told you, racing off—"

"SARGE!"

"WHAT?" Enraged, Sarge spun on Clever and glared. "What?"

Clever couldn't speak. All he could do was point a shaking finger towards Weebit, who was heading in their direction at a leisurely stroll. He was still several metres from where they stood under the plant, following the aerial dance of a butterfly with enchanted eyes. But it wasn't the merrily wandering Weebit that Clever was pointing at. It was the raven. A large black raven, flying low behind him and creating a speeding shadow on the ground, unblinking eyes locked onto its target. Gliding silently on spread wings it swooped towards the earth.

"*WEEBIT!*" Sarge managed to scream. "*RUN!*"

All Clever could do was gurgle. His throat caught and he watched in horror as the raven dipped. Weebit was snatched up in its beak, his body swinging crazily as the bird beat its wings against the grass and lifted. Clever felt the air move past his face as the raven swept up over the garden, its prize dangling against a feathered chest. All Clever could see was that sharp beak wrapped into Weebit's clothes.

"NO!" Clever glanced at the others, and then realised the cry had come from him. He spun to keep his eyes on the raven and Weebit, his mind still screaming over and over. No, no, no! They couldn't lose Weebit. Not now, not here. They couldn't. In the back of his mind, Clever registered that Peter had heard the commotion and was turning to see what was going on, but his focus was set on the bird. He mustn't take his eyes off Weebit. As if in slow motion in the background, Peter spun away from the human model. Clever wasn't exactly sure what happened next. He knew the raven was flying away. He was responsible for the group and he had let a predator snatch Weebit away from them. He felt the weight of it crush his chest. And then—

Peter kept spinning, his ladder bucked sideways, and he was launched into the air along with a bucket that flew after him. He flung his hands out, grasping desperately. His whole body twisting, he arced out from the model, arms whirling and struck the bird a solid blow as it flew past. In a flurry of wings, feathers and enraged squawking the raven succeeded in righting itself mid-air – but it dropped Weebit! He tumbled and landed in the garden surrounding the model, sending up a tiny plume of soil. The raven landed on the nearby roof, screeching a bitter protest from where it landed. Peter crunched into the surrounding pebbled road, throwing his hands out to break his fall. The ladder clattered behind him, and the bucket landed on his hip, splashing dirty liquid all over him and the ground. Clever couldn't help but gape at the whole scene.

"Stay here, Nimin," commanded Sarge. A pale Nimin nodded.

Clever was still gawping when Sarge grabbed his arm and pulled him across towards the base of the model's garden. They kept a wary eye on the raven, which was still perched on the roof of the building, chattering in disgust and ruffling its feathers. When Weebit's crookedly smiling face bobbed up over the edge Clever breathed out his relief, shrugged his arm back from Sarge, and dashed over to Peter.

"Are you all right?"

Peter winced as he rolled over and sat up, but he looked as if he would live. Clever looked back to double-check that Weebit was okay. He watched Sarge scale the stone edging with ease, hoist Weebit up by his armpits, check his eyes with a slowly moving finger, and nod in satisfaction. Clever wondered how Weebit's eyes had followed Sarge's finger, given they would be hard pressed to do it normally. He snorted. Then bit his lip and grimaced, hoping Sarge hadn't heard. Now was not the time for snorting. He turned his attention back to Peter. One knee was dribbling blood down his leg, and both palms were sliced and bleeding and covered in dirt, but he had fallen a long way without acquiring too much damage. Peter seemed more unhappy about getting wet. He looked down at his soaked clothes and shook his head in disgust.

"Yerghh." He went to swipe his hip with a palm, thought better of it, and glanced back towards the model instead. "Is Weebit all right? Yes? Good. I'm going inside to get patched up. I'll see you guys later?"

Clever nodded and stammered his thanks. His heart was still pounding, he couldn't believe what had just happened, and all he wanted to do was get them all back to the new Dingledell safely. He looked up at Sarge, noticing the considering expression on his face as he watched Peter limp towards the building. When Sarge returned his gaze and nodded in the direction of home he knew, for now at least, they agreed on one thing.

CHAPTER FIVE

Clever swallowed gingerly and then blinked. The mushrooms were delicious. It was the first meal he could remember Nimin cooking that he would describe as edible, and it was really very good. Nimin had been reluctant to dish up the mushrooms that, he said, nearly got Weebit eaten. They had finally convinced him that he wasn't at fault any more than Clever or Sarge, and probably less so, and eventually he had excitedly crashed about in the cooking pit with his pots and pans. Clever glanced over at Sarge and nodded in agreement when Sarge's eyebrows shot up to meet his hair. Both dipped their spoons back into their bowls and raced to finish so they could have another helping.

"Your human moved fast," said Sarge, looking at Clever over his raised spoon. He slurped appreciatively, peered down at his nearly empty bowl, raised it up to his mouth and drank, then held the bowl out to Nimin to ask for more. Nimin's eyes widened in surprise and, almost falling off his stool in his haste, he leapt to his feet and raced to refill the bowl. He was so delighted, he might as well have floated to his cooking pot. It was likely he had never been asked for seconds before.

"I am intrigued, I'll admit. I did not know that humans could move so fast," said Sarge. He took his bowl back from Nimin with a nod of thanks and slurped again from his spoon. "It could make him more dangerous, of course, but perhaps he may be useful to us. He was helpful today."

Clever looked at Sarge suspiciously, but he seemed to be speaking plainly and thoughtfully. Clever thought about the events of the day and wondered about Peter's speed. He had never seen a human move like that in all of his hours of research. He also had a suspicion that Peter had not seen the bird and hadn't intended to throw himself at it, but that was how it had appeared. Maybe he would ask Peter about it at some future point, but in the meantime he wasn't going to say anything about his doubts to Sarge, and he would take this new attitude towards Peter as the welcome gift it was. Although, he thought, maybe it is the effect of the mushrooms. He sniffed at his bowl. Maybe the mushrooms are making Sarge sound reasonable for once. Maybe they are magical mushrooms.

Very early the next morning, Clever watched as Sarge surveyed Dingledell with thoughtful eyes and then sauntered out of the cavern. Sarge had said nothing further about the woods for their new home the previous night, and he wasn't giving away his thoughts this morning. Clever waited for a few beats before he checked Weebit and Nimin, both still snoring, and followed as quietly as he could. He skulked from tree to tree, keeping an eye on Sarge, but not daring to get too close. Where was he going? Clever maintained his distance as they wound their way through the trees, heading towards where they had first entered the woods the day they arrived. Sarge didn't seem to be looking for anything – he looked as if he was out for a pleasurable stroll. He reached the open, checked for golfers and motored across to the bushes surrounding the fishes pond. Clever also made sure the coast was clear, peered to see where Sarge was, and followed.

He scuttled from bush to bush until he found where Sarge was sitting – by nearly stepping on him. Clever gasped and reeled back but Sarge didn't appear to hear him, focusing on unwinding a line and hook. He put something onto the hook and tossed the line into the water, then leaned back against a rock and sighed contentedly.

Clever couldn't believe it. For someone who disliked the area Sarge was making himself right at home. Clever watched for several minutes, confused by Sarge and wondering what he was really up to. Sarge appeared to gaze into the water, a small smile playing around his lips, and then he squinted up at the bright sky and roved his eyes over the surrounding greenery. Clever wasn't sure, but he had the feeling Sarge was falling for the place, picturing himself here when he had a spare moment to catch fishes.

Something tugged at the line and Sarge was galvanised into action. He gently pulled on the line, and Clever excitedly glanced towards the water where an orange flash near the surface indicated Sarge's success. Clever wanted to stay and watch the battle, but he knew it wouldn't take Sarge long to land his fish, and then he would likely head straight back to Dingledell. Clever backed up quietly, spun around and headed home at a brisk pace, figuring he would have a bit of time to enjoy his walk back, while also aware that Sarge wouldn't be far behind him.

When he was almost home, he felt the urge to pause behind a tree root to see if Sarge was going to be long. It was a lucky thing that he did, because Sarge had pulled in the fish faster than Clever had assumed. He was trotting towards where Clever hid behind his tree, carefully balancing the fish over a shoulder. Boggit, thought Clever, he wouldn't be able to get back to Dingledell ahead of Sarge. All he could do was hold still and hope that he wasn't caught in the act of spying.

Sarge casually jogged past the other side of the tree. Clever held his breath while he passed, and then he held it a bit longer while he listened for the muted shuffled pine needles sound of Sarge's footfalls. When he couldn't hear his movements any longer, Clever let himself relax, releasing his breath slowly. Now he would head home and just pretend he had stepped out for a few minutes—

"Good morning, Clever."

Clever squeaked and jumped, then rolled his eyes at Sarge, who was leaning against the tree with his arms folded over his chest, the fish lying on the ground behind him. He was smirking.

"You know, you should keep to being a scientist. You do know that, don't you?"

Clever rolled his eyes again and tried a glare, but words failed him.

"I've been thinking—" said Sarge.

"Mmmm?"

"It's on your head to control the human."

Sarge was agreeing to stay, Clever told himself, trying not to smile. He would be able to continue his research on Peter. Excellent! He couldn't help it, he grinned and nodded eagerly.

"First thing, though, I'm going to enjoy eliminating that bird," said Sarge, with a determined look. He smiled at the thought. "Then, I think, we can secure the woods and get on with making this our new home."

He picked up the fish and walked off towards Dingledell. "I wonder if there's any mushrooms left to go with our breakfast."

Clever waited until Sarge was several steps ahead and then took the opportunity to punch the air. Yes! He plastered a serious look on his face and raced after Sarge.

#

It was several days later, and Clever was thrilled with their progress. He looked around the cavern with a satisfied air and sighed happily. Dingledell had continued to be transformed into something even better than he had ever dreamed. He walked up a main flight of stairs leading into the trunk, turning his head as he passed smaller flights of stairs, all leading off towards future chambers that would be carved out higher up the tree. Weebit had planned and they had built the first lookout, a small chamber far enough up the trunk that it was above the lowest branches and several metres above the ground below.

Clever stepped out of the opening of the lookout onto a specially carved area on the branch adjoining the doorway. He was feeling very proud of their efforts and fully aware that as the assignment leader he would get a big share of the recognition. The old Dingledell didn't have a balcony branch, complete with safety barriers. He smiled at the leaves rustling just outside his reach, dreaming of a Dingledell ceremony where one of the chambers would be named after him. Maybe the new lookout? That would show the others! He leaned against the barrier and peered down at the pine needles below. While he was dreaming, he thought, he might as well pretend the elders named the main cavern after him. He smirked again and turned his back to the barrier so he could look towards the doorway. Weebit had even designed a roof of sorts from a piece of curved bark, which was supported over the doorway and designed to protect a part of the balcony from the rain.

Clever's smile widened at the memory of the previous night's meal. They had celebrated their new home with the last of the mushrooms, saved specially, and a final touch had been put in place when he had hung a beautifully carved piece of wood near the main entrance spelling out '*Dingledell*'. As far as they were concerned, it was now officially their new home. They still needed to complete a network of tunnels throughout the roots, finish the trunk stairways and build more chambers coming off the passageways, but he knew Weebit was happy with the work to date and was merrily planning the layout to allow for further expansions. Weebit really was an artist. He had even had them laying out and locking together different coloured wood shavings on the main cavern floor, which made little sense until about halfway through the job, when Clever could see a picture forming. The Dinglemen would spend the next several generations walking over butterflies. Butterflies perched on leaves, butterflies in flight, and two butterflies over near the cooking pit that were either dancing together or duelling, depending on your mood when you looked at them. As Nimin had said, this Dingledell was going to be maximal. He wandered back down the main stairs, filling his lungs with the smell of fresh pine as he went.

Nimin was so excited about the new lookout he convinced the others to drag their bedding up there for the night, so they could "watch the stars while they slept." They were all in a good mood, so nobody pointed out that you couldn't sleep and watch stars at the same time, even though Clever was itching to say so. Torture wouldn't get him to admit it, but he was just as excited as Nimin about sleeping next to the new balcony.

#

It was late. The stars had been out for hours and had been brief entertainment for the Dinglemen, before the others got bored with staring at unmoving shiny spots and had gone to sleep. The only sounds to upset the still night were snoring from Sarge, Weebit and Nimin. Clever had his cushion folded around his ears, a permanent frown marking his forehead while he tossed from side to side. It had occurred to him that the move to a higher perch and fresh air might have stopped them from snoring quite so much as usual. Unfortunately, if anything, he thought it made them all worse. He didn't have a hope of getting to sleep. Clever concentrated on their snoring instead, listening for nuances amongst the snorts and burbles. Nimin was the quiet snorer, gently snuffling and blowing bubbles, Sarge didn't so much snore as wheeze with the odd snort, and Weebit, by far the smallest of the group, constantly rumbled from deep within his body, sounding a lot like a train going past on rusted metal tracks.

"Drongles," Clever muttered.

He huffed out his frustration and wiggled his way out of his bedding to stand on the balcony. It was cool for a summer night, and clear, with a three-quarter moon shining a silver path through the leaves. He looked over the barrier to where the moonlight gently lit patches of pine needles layered well beneath him, surprised that from his height he could still see a lone insect as it toiled across the ground. He relaxed and watched the insect, once again smiling at their good luck in finding this new home.

All of a sudden, his spot on the branch didn't feel so peaceful. He felt the hairs on his neck bristle. Despite the gentle night, he could feel something, an atmosphere of menace, as if there was someone or something watching him. Scanning the branches and leaves at eye level, he didn't see anything out of place. Nothing appeared to be moving.

"Psst."

Clever spun towards the lookout opening,

where Sarge was urgently gesturing for him to come back inside. Clever raced across the balcony and into the doorway, feeling a gust of air behind him. A flapping of wings and a '*whoosh*' told Clever how close he had come to being bird food. The moonlight allowed him to see the raven land on a branch of a neighbouring tree, only a short distance away from where they stood. The bird was watching the doorway, turning its head from side to side as if listening, flat eyes blinking at them. Not that Clever was surprised if it *was* listening. Behind him, the volume was still set at a loud racket, with a steady rhythm between Nimin and Weebit's snores.

"nnggh—pfeww—nnggh—pffeew—"

"bbrrfff—pft—nrk—"

The raven hopped across from its branch to land on the balcony, making Clever squeak in horror and step back on Sarge's foot.

"Boggit, get off!"

"Sorry, sorry," said Clever. He stepped sideways and glanced up at Sarge's face. In the moonlight, he could make out his happily determined expression.

"You set this up!"

"How would I have been able to set this

up?"

"All right then, you expected it."

"Yup."

"I could have been killed!"

"And yet you're still here, annoying me."

Clever couldn't think of a reply. The raven had put an unblinking eye right up against the opening and he was mesmerised by the black ink of the pupil.

"C'mon, come on," muttered Sarge.

Clever squeaked again and backed up farther. The raven took its head away from the doorway and replaced the eye with a sharp beak. One quick twist, and the bark covering was broken back so it could reach into the opening. The beak opened wide around where Sarge stood, he did a quick duck and side step, and Clever closed his eyes. He couldn't watch. He heard Sarge say, "Hello, birdie," a smacking sound, and then a thump.

"brrrzt—" Nimin broke off mid-snore and woke to see what was happening. "Oh good, the bad birdie is gone," he said, yawned and rolled back to sleep.

Sarge lay back down on his bedding, put his pick near his side, stretched out, and in less than a minute started snoring again.

Weebit hadn't woken up.

"nnnggh—pf—"

"eez—nnrrk."

Clever glared at their sleeping forms, then he moved his bedding to the back of the lookout, near the stairs, and lay down. He pulled his cushion back over his ears and muttered to himself about loud-mouthed drongles who wouldn't be missed if they all got eaten.

CHAPTER SIX

On Christmas day, Peter's parents gave him a small pastel picture of a Sopwith Camel in flight. He hung it up in his bedroom over his desk. His sock drawer was replenished for the next year, he ate junk food until he felt queasy, and as usual it had been a quiet morning spent with his parents. After lunch though, he carried a small mountain of leftovers to the Dinglemen and spent a happy half hour sitting under the trees trying to explain the reason behind the holiday to Clever.

"So, let me get this correct. It is the birthday of a human called Jesus, and everybody else gets the presents?"

"Yup."

"Really? What did he do?"

"Er, I think he was a carpenter."

"Is that right? So this would be the same as

all of the other Dinglemen getting presents to celebrate the ageing of Weebit?" Clever snorted and broke into a cackle. "And what happened to him?"

"Well, er, he was killed." Peter's answers were deliberately simple. He had a good idea how easily Clever's mind could mangle religion.

"Why, was he a poor carpenter?"

"I don't think so."

"Hmm, well at least you are all celebrating his birth, not his death."

"Oh no, that's Easter," Peter blurted, before mentally slapping his head. Idiot, he thought. He saw the look on Clever's face and decided now was a really good time to change the subject.

"Let me tell you about my presents."

Nimin came over from where he had been attacking the pile of food. So far, Peter had seen him gobble pieces from the fruit pudding, the banana cake, the vanilla slice, the cherry slice, the piece of turkey leg, the chocolate muffin, the apple pie, the potato chips and the party pies. What had been an impressive pile of food now had a sagging look about it. Weebit and Sarge were being a lot more refined and sat comfortably at the side of the pile, sampling small pieces and making suggestions about what tasted good and what to try next.

"Why is the food green and red? How did they make it such pretty colours? How can I do that to our food? Is it a trick of some sort? What's added to the food? What happens when you mix the green and red? And what are these?" asked Nimin, thrusting out a fistful of crumbs. He wobbled on his feet and grabbed at Peter's leg to stay upright.

"Food colouring," said Peter. "And that *was* a fairy cake."

"*Fairy* cake! Fairy cake! I've eaten fairy cake. Ooh, that makes me a *fairy*!"

Sarge looked up from where he was sitting, frowned, and came over to stand near Clever, who was studying Nimin with a puzzled expression.

"What's up with you?" asked Sarge.

Peter peered closely at Nimin as well, noticing something wasn't quite right about the look on his face. Nimin's large smile was crooked, muscles twitched in his cheeks and his bloodshot eyes twirled and flickered.

"*Fairies can fly*! I'll need a cape, Clever, so

you'll all know I can fly!" Nimin barrelled off through the trees, whooping as he went, "Fly, Fly!"

Sarge took one look after Nimin, then looked up at Peter. "I think you should explain."

"I think he's had a reaction to the food colouring. Basically, um, in effect, that is, he's on a bit of a high," said Peter. "It should wear off," he added, apologetically.

Sarge's mouth twisted into a smile. "Right then, it serves the inkblot right for being such a glut."

There was another loud '*whoopee*' from within the trees. Sarge's smile widened into a grin. "Best I catch him before he tests out his flying theory." He sped into the trees in the direction of the sounds of merriment.

#

Peter sat out on the back steps of his home to watch the twilight creep in, a cold can of lemonade dribbling condensation in his hand, his eyes unfocused and his mind wandering. He ran the fingers of his free hand over the hard wood of the painted green steps beneath him and wondered if people really did get piles by sitting on hard surfaces for too long, and if so, why did schools have hard chairs? Maybe the education department was given kickbacks by a haemorrhoid cream company? He shook his head, sighed contentedly and shifted his thoughts to the events of the day, smiling at the memory of Nimin whooping and zigzagging through the trees. Somehow, Clever had succeeded in talking Sarge into staying in the woods, and Peter couldn't have been happier about it.

He lifted his eyes to watch his mother working in her small vegetable garden, his gaze following her as she moved between the short rows of tomato plants, lettuces, carrots and cucumbers, crooning to the plants and talking out her idea for her next piece of artwork. Something about a miniature horse, he thought he heard. Which brought his thoughts back to the Dinglemen. Even Sarge was nicer to him. Not friendly exactly, but not hostile either, and Peter thought that was quite an achievement.

He smiled again and stood to throw his empty drink can into the recycling bin, making him think briefly of Daisy. She was the summer cook's little sister and was at school with Peter. The tougher kids in their class called her Daisychain, but never to her face. She was famed for lecturing on the finer points of saving the environment and for throwing lemonade cans at her neighbour when he put them into the rubbish bin instead of the recycling. Peter always wondered how her older sister, Caitlin, who filled in the cook's job for the summer while he went off to slaughter rare butterflies for his collection, got away with driving the car that she did without constant nagging from Daisy. Caitlin had a beaten up used-to-be pink VW Beetle that looked, even last year, like the engine was held together by rubber bands, superglue and cobwebs. It smoked a bit.

#

A visit to Peter's house! Clever was having difficulty maintaining his composure as the Dinglemen walked through the trees to their meeting place just inside the woods to wait for Peter. Nimin could hardly be contained, and even Sarge couldn't hide the fact he was looking forward to the afternoon's activity. He crossed his arms and slouched against a tree, but Clever knew he was excited in spite of himself. Even Weebit's wild red hair was electrified, and that usually only happened when he had one of his tools in his hands and a task ahead of him. Peter had told them he would come to get them when he finished work and would explain his idea, which was going to allow them to see the golf course from the air. He had said they should be able to see all around the grounds and over the woods to the river and even parts of the surrounding city. Clever couldn't wait to see the plan. He heard someone walking along the trees, checked to see that it was Peter, and leapt out to accost him.

"Good, you're here. I insist we observe this plan straight away," said Clever, trying to hide his excitement, but only managing to sound pompous.

Peter smiled at him. "It's pronounced *plane*," he said.

"Yes, yes. Jolly good. Let's see it. This flying contraption called a *plaanne*," said Clever.

"Come on then. Let's go, and I'll show you." Peter led off across the grounds, with

Nimin skipping around his heels, and Clever and Sarge only just managing to saunter behind them. They all walked along the side of what Peter called fairway fifteen, then cut through the trees at the end and popped out near one of the circles of short grass. Peter had told Clever that they were called 'greens', but he couldn't really see why. They didn't look that much greener than the surrounding grass, and he had suggested to Peter that 'shorts' would be a more apt name for them.

They had all been so caught up in their discussion about the plane that they hadn't noticed two humans, paused halfway along the fairway while one took a frustrated swipe at the grass. Clever had already marched out across the shorter grass of the green, when he heard a muffled '*toc*' sound. He panicked and froze, staring at the others to see what they would do. Sarge and Nimin were already speeding back under the trees to join Weebit, who had been bringing up the rear as usual, and Peter didn't need to hide. He just stepped backward a few paces. Clever started to run towards the others but a white missile crashed into the earth in his path. He gasped and veered to the side, then spied a small hole that was much closer than the trees and raced for it, diving head first into the ground. It wasn't until he stood up that he realised it wasn't like any other hole he had ever encountered. The walls were smooth and white and there was a pole that travelled upward from the centre. He put a hand on the pole and looked up towards the opening. It was at least three times over his head, and he couldn't see anything above him but a gently waving white flag, blue sky and part of a cloud. Clever couldn't tell how far away the humans were but calculated they would be close, so he hunched at the bottom, sighed, leaned against the pole and waited for them to pass by. He heard a thump on the ground a few metres away from his hole and wondered how long he would have to remain trapped.

"Where's Clever?" he heard Peter hiss. He opened his mouth to shout, but just as he did he heard Peter raise his voice and call "hello" to the humans. Clever sighed again.

"I'll get the flag for you!" he heard Peter call. Peter's face loomed over his hole, blocking off his view of flag and sky.

"Cover your head!" Peter whispered.

From Clever's viewpoint, Peter looked as if

he was pursing crooked lips and was being apologetic, or found something hilarious, or both. He didn't think his predicament was very funny. Then Peter gripped the pole and lifted it out, leaving him more room to spread his arms. Cover his head, he thought. Why would he need to do that? A second later the ground above vibrated, his light was cut off and a white ball fell in on top of him.

"Boggit!"

"Sorry mate, did you say something?" was the muffled question from one of the humans. He heard Peter reply, then his hand reached in and fished out the ball. Peter peered in quickly, and Clever spread his hands and bugged out his eyes to say 'get me out of here'. Peter grimaced and then, once again, he was gone. Clever gritted his teeth. He couldn't believe this was happening to him! He would never hear the end of it, and he was sure Sarge would tell everyone when they went back to get them from the old Dingledell. He would be the laughing stock. Well, anyway, more than usual. Clever heard a smacking sound and covered his head with his arms. He felt the ball rolling towards his hole, suddenly deciding then that he was not going to accept having dimply white balls land on him. He pushed his hands up and jumped to meet the ball, making it jig back out of his hole and roll away. Ha, take that, he thought.

"Drat, that was close. I was sure I had it," said a voice. Clever strained his ears and wasn't disappointed when he heard another smack. He sighed. The golf balls were not going to stop until he let them land on him and stay there. He was not happy. Once again, he heard a '*toc*' and braced for the next ball. Then he waited, waited a bit more, and finally peered up towards the sky when the ball didn't come.

"Aw rats," said the voice, "I'm not having a very good game at all, am I?"

At the bottom of his hole, Clever groaned. If he had to be subjected to white balls landing on him, the very least that could happen is for the human to get on with it. How hard was it to smack a defenseless little ball into a hole in the ground, anyway? Another, closer '*toc*', and the ball thumped in on top of him.

"Oof."

Once again, Peter took the ball off his shoulders, peering in to check on Clever, who took the opportunity to make a rude gesture while he had the chance. Peter smiled and was gone yet again. Clever grimaced and hoped that was the end of the dimply ball business. He listened to the voices, not hearing what they were saying, but glad they were moving away. What felt like several long minutes later, and the heads of Nimin, Sarge, and Weebit peered over the lip of his hole to see how he had fared. Only Sarge had a straight face, and his deadpan expression looked like glass under stress, ready to crack at any moment.

"It's okay, they're gone," said Peter, looking in over the others.

"Okay?" spluttered Clever, as he clambered out from the bottom. "Okay, is it? He says it's okay! I could have been squashed. I had golf balls land on me. Golf balls! Oh, the indignity. I might be injured. Am I injured anywhere? I can't believe this happened to *me*. This is *NOT* funny! Hey!"

As a group, the other Dinglemen had already walked off, with Nimin waving his hands about and yapping excitedly about the plane. Clever muttered under his breath but trailed after them. He glared up at the grinning Peter, walking beside him.

#

Peter's parents were both out the back of the house. He shouted "hello" to them, and then led the Dinglemen down the short hallway to his room and ushered them through the door. The model plane was sitting on his desk opposite the doorway.

"Ooh! Maximal!"

"Oh, sterling!" said Clever. Weebit squeaked excitedly, his eyebrows waggling.

"Hmm. Tell me again, that thing flies?" said Sarge.

In an instant, the Dinglemen scaled a desk leg to stand on the desktop with the plane. With its large wing span, both wings hung over the edges of the desk and the body of the plane took up most of the surface. Peter ran a hand along the tail section while the Dinglemen clambered up onto the nearest wing to peer into the two seats. They were walking on a wing painted a bright yellow, with a black strip near the body as if to show passengers where to walk, while the body of the plane was a dark blue with a red stripe, the number seventeen emblazoned on the sides and again near the nose.

"Weeee." Nimin awkwardly slid down the wing to land clumsily on his feet. He raced around to the front of the plane, where he banged his head on the silver prop connected to the nose, "Ow, oops, whoopsie." He staggered briefly, giggled, and then headed around to clamber back onto the wing to rejoin Sarge, who frowned at him and checked his eyes for any suspicious whirling. Clever had climbed down to glance along the length of the plane, nodding appreciatively at the graceful sloping from the nose to the tail.

"I figure she'll go up easily with one of you in her," said Peter. He caressed the plane again, earning himself a calculating look from Clever.

"We'll have, maybe, ten to fifteen minutes on each flight, and you'll get a birds-eye view of the whole golf course and some of the surrounding streets. You will be able to look *down* on the trees. It'll be great."

"You mean, we'd be airgonauts?"

"Er, yeah. Flying, right? Yeah."

"She?" asked Clever, "You just called it a *she*."

"Yeah. We tend to call planes and cars *she*." Peter thought for a minute. "Actually, it might just be a guy thing." The Dinglemen immediately looked to their femmes expert for his opinion on the sex of the plane. Weebit gave it a considering look, walking around the whole of the plane while rubbing his chin. He looked through under the wing at Clever and gave his professional opinion.

"Nah."

Peter smiled and shrugged. He was like any hobby enthusiast and couldn't shut up once he had an interested audience, or any audience for that matter. While he had the Dinglemen listening to him, he was going to share as much as he possibly could. "This is a perfectly scaled down model of the real plane, which was used to train pilots during the Second World War to prepare them to fly more advanced aircraft. See this little tail wheel? It's steerable, so I have really good control during take-off and landing. I've also put in a powerful—"

This was far too much information for the others and they wandered around the plane, giving the tail an exploratory rub, testing the tyres – Nimin by sitting on one and Sarge by kicking the other – leaving hand prints all over the prop and sliding down the sloping wings. Weebit was slouching in the front seat and might have been making '*vrroom vrroom*' noises. Clever was still firing questions at Peter.

"What's it made out of?"

"Light woods called balsa and plywood, to keep the weight down, and there are some fiberglass parts."

"How do you control it?"

"I have a radio with four channels on the ground, with a transmitter, and the plane has four servos, so I can direct it to do acrobatics. You know, loops, and stall turns and barrel rolls. But we won't be doing any of that stuff anyway, you might fall out. Peter guessed that Clever didn't know all of the jargon, but he must have got the gist of it because he was starting to tinge green.

"And—" Clever's voice came out squeaky, and he cleared his throat. "Ahem, and how fast will it be going with one of us in it?"

"Oh, I can get it to fly really, really slowly, practically hover over the trees. Trust me."

Peter was still raving to a more and more disinterested looking Clever, about wing area, fuselage length and flying weight, when they heard a commotion from the shelf above the desk.

#

Sarge, Nimin and Weebit had quickly become bored with the plane and had climbed up a convenient lamp to check out what was on the shelf. They had discovered the smurf figurines that Peter collected when he was younger. The commotion had been caused by Weebit knocking over some of the figurines as he made a beeline towards the back row and his throwing an apology over a shoulder at the fallen smurfs.

"Forgive me, sorry."

Peter watched as Nimin came face to face with the first smurf in his path. It held a packet of yellow french-fries in one hand, and a single fry held out in the other, as if offering it to a friend. Nimin's eyes lit up at the sight of the fries, but then suspicion crept across his face and he leaned forward to sniff at them. He frowned and cocked his head, considering the figure in front of him. Peter bit his lip as he watched Nimin testing the outstretched fry, his frown deepening into a scowl as he confirmed that it really wasn't food. The usually equable and easy-going Nimin scowled at the grinning smurf, prodded the outstretched arm and then poked the smurf in the face. Peter strangled a laugh and looked between the figurines for Sarge and Weebit.

Sarge had somehow managed to get in the middle of a kung-fu smurf, a pirate smurf with a threatening sword, and a cowboy smurf that was holding a whip. He squared up to the pirate.

"Are you eye-balling me?" he roared. His glaring eyes shifted from one potential assailant to the next. Sarge clearly decided to finish the fight before they had any chance to attack. In a blur, he threw a sharp jab-cross combination at the head of the pirate, did a complicated back kick at the kung-fu smurf, and lined up the cowboy for a few swift punches before a final spinning round kick knocked the cowboy over. The kung-fu and cowboy smurfs had both toppled, but by some miraculous chance the pirate was still wobbling on its feet. Sarge's eyes narrowed and he squared his chest up to the pirate.

"Still got some yike in you, eh?"

He exploded into action and finished off

his last adversary with a jumping knee aimed at the stomach. The figurine scattered its neighbours. Sarge stepped back and glared around at his slain enemies, visibly disgusted at their lack of fighting ability and stamina. Then he turned to smirk at Peter and grin at Clever, who had just climbed onto the shelf to see what was going on. Sarge looked so smug Peter didn't have the heart to tell him he had just beaten up some plastic toys.

Clever was inspecting the smurfs. He came nose to nose with a hiker smurf and peered at its face, then frowned and waved his hand in front of its staring eyes.

"They're not moving. They look frozen solid. Hmmm." He cocked his head and rubbed his chin, then stepped back and surveyed the frozen masses, taking in the blank, vacant eyes. Clever visibly flinched.

"Aaaahhhhh!" he screamed, waving a pointed finger at the smurfs and then jabbing it in Peter's direction. "Murderer! What did you do to them? Did you *freeze* them? They're *blue*! How *could* you?"

Peter stared at Clever's waving finger and horrified face, his mind racing and his lips pressed together. How could he explain this?

The finger was still waving accusatorily, and Sarge had spun to scowl at him. It looked as if there was no way around it. He was going to have to tell them.

"They're plastic."

"Plastic?"

Peter nodded. "Look closer."

"They're plastic!"

There was a pregnant pause.

"That's sick!"

"They're collectibles. From a cartoon show. They're toys."

"You mean, I just pummelled a couple of plastic toys?" asked Sarge, exchanging looks with Clever. He glanced around at the carnage he had left and smirked. "I thought that was too easy. They were a bunch of cream puffs."

The first thing Peter noticed was that Clever's face was flushed pink, his lips pressed together. Then both Clever and Sarge couldn't hold their laughter any longer. Even Nimin was grinning at Peter as Clever pointed at his face and hooted in glee.

"Got you! I can't believe you fell for that!"

Sarge was doubled over with laughter. He put a hand back to steady himself but missed the nearest smurf and stumbled backward over the pirate.

"Very sorry! I didn't mean to hurt you!" He wailed into laughter again and sat hard onto the stomach of the kung-fu smurf, patting the figurine and shaking his head as he tried to stop laughing.

"Oh, well done. Very funny," Peter said, flushed with embarrassment. He smiled ruefully. "Yes, fine, you got me."

Sarge had nearly calmed down but hiccupped and snorted, which set him off laughing again. Peter couldn't help grinning back at him.

"You know, it's getting late. We'll take the plane out in the next couple of days, I promise. You guys should get home before it gets too dark."

"You're absolutely correct," said Clever, falling back into sounding pompous. Sarge snorted again and smirked at him.

"Where's Weebit?" asked Clever.

Weebit was happy. Weebit had just met smurfette.

"Charmed, I'm sure," he said, bowing at his waist. "Please, forgive me for being so forward, but I must tell you, I find you to be the most beautiful creature I have ever laid my eyes upon. Such glorious flowing yellow hair, such delicate features, and madam, that pointy hat looks just delightful on you. You take my breath away, darling. May I call you darling?"

Peter's eyebrows rose. If a piece of plastic could be flattered into blushing, smurfette would be pink by now. The other Dinglemen had overheard Weebit and worked their way between the rows of figurines to where he stood.

"Um, Weebit? You know she's not real?" said Clever.

"Weebit, we have to get home," said Sarge.

"Madam, forgive me. I must away. But I shall never forget your enchanting beauty. I shall take your cherished image with me forever, burned into my mind and branded into my heart."

"See, I told you he was good," hissed Clever at Peter.

Weebit kissed smurfette gently on the forehead. Then, head held high, he swept an imaginary cape about his shoulders and strode off into the distance. Peter caught him as he fell off the shelf.

CHAPTER SEVEN

The Dinglemen made their way from Dingledell to the edge of the woods. Clever scurried with the others, Nimin talking in his ear and Sarge forcing them to march, until they skidded to a halt at Peter's feet. Today, they were going to lunch with more than two hundred humans. Peter smiled a greeting and turned to lead them towards the clubrooms, explaining as they walked that he had already prepared a hidey-hole for them. He had fixed the tablecloths so they would hang all the way down to the carpet to give them cover under one of the tables of food, and he had also placed a cardboard box they could hide in under the table for extra cover, just in case anyone looked, and he had punched an opening in the side so they would be able to move freely in and out of the box.

As they walked across the sun dappled

grass, he offered to smuggle food off the table, but Sarge said they would be fine to help themselves. Nimin looked very happy at the idea of a table loaded with human food.

"Will any of the food be coloured?" asked Clever, eyeing Nimin's thrilled expression, and earning an amused hoot from Sarge.

They walked past one of those *greens* circles and Clever narrowed his eyes at the little hole with the flag sticking out of it. Sarge noticed what he was looking at and grinned, but it was too nice a day and his ribbing was only half-hearted. The only time Sarge frowned was when he was asked to climb into a shoebox for Peter to smuggle them into the club. Then his good humour slipped.

"This is embarrassing," grumbled Sarge. "If anyone tells that I was carried around by a human, there will be *consequences*." He glared at each of the others before roughly clambering into the box.

Humans were everywhere. Seated at the round tables, standing in groups near the walls, leaning against the drinks bar, wandering up and down past their hiding spot, and walking through the doorway just behind the tables. There were legs of all descriptions passing by. Clever was in research heaven. He wished Peter could fit under the table with them, so he could fire questions about the legs. Why were some teetering by on spiky shoes, for example? He saw one pair of especially high spikes and noticed that the toetips were painted red. Red! He really needed Peter under here. As if on cue, Peter crouched down beside where he stood and the cloth was moved just enough for a hand to push two small, warm pies past him – Dinglemen sized pies.

Clever managed to rasp out, "Red toetips!" and caught a glimpse of a smile before Peter stood and his legs moved away.

"Red toetips," Clever muttered to himself.

The next half hour passed in a flurry of legs and noise. Clever noted that more and more of the humans remained seated, fewer coming up to collect food off the table above him. This made it easier for Weebit and Nimin, who mostly stayed under the box but went out on food runs when they had finished their current supply. They alternated who did the foraging, each brushing past Clever with a determined air on their way out and squeezing past him with hands full upon their return.

Each time, he could hear enthusiastic murmuring from the box while they sampled what had been chosen and delivered. Between them, they had made several trips and didn't look to be slowing down any time soon, and so far neither had noticed that he had pinched a few mouthfuls off their load as they passed, or at least, neither minded enough to comment. Sarge alternated between the revelry inside the box and Clever's position with the view of the humans at the tables and around the room.

Clever and Sarge swapped glances when an older human in a suit, an overweight male, stood at the front of the room and used a finger to tap a black cone-shaped object that was attached to a tall metal stick. A whining noise spread through the room, making them wince and cover their ears. The fat man fiddled with the black cone and then spoke into it, his voice loud enough to be heard easily from the back of the room. Clever wondered how the cone could spread his voice around and made a mental note to ask Peter about it. Ten minutes later, the man's speech was still droning, Sarge was back in the box with the others, and Clever was trying not to yawn. It was then that he noticed the fat man kept glancing towards the door behind their table and scowling at whoever was standing there. Clever put his head inside the box, motioned for Sarge to join him, and together they moved to peer out from under the cloth at the rear of the table.

Two humans, dressed in matching khaki tunics, black shorts and mud-covered solid work boots were loitering in the doorway. There all similarities ended – one of them was wide, squat and built like a tree trunk and the other was a walking twig. Neither looked as if they belonged in the room of spiky shoes, and they definitely didn't look like any of the humans that smacked balls past the woods. These two didn't look as if they would indulge in ball hitting, thought Clever. What was the right word? Soft? Puffy. They didn't look puffy enough. The fat man finished his speech to the sound of clapping hands, and then he walked straight towards the two humans in the doorway, nodded a curt greeting and squeezed out between them, disappearing from Clever's view. The two humans exchanged glances and followed in his wake.

Clever was just considering joining the

others when Peter knelt by the rear of the table and placed the shoebox down for them to make their escape, tapping on the party box with a finger to let the others know it was time to leave. Several minutes of being carried later, and Peter placed the box on the ground to let them out, blinking, into the sunlight.

"That was so maximal! Man, am I full. Woheee!" Nimin had what looked like coconut flakes down his front. Weebit was still chewing and grinned a blue mush. Sarge glanced at Nimin's tunic. "Nimin, you are a glut. What are you?"

"A very happy glut."

"You could have let us out sooner, you know," Sarge grumbled at Peter. "Being carried around in a box is humiliating."

"Sorry."

"Interesting. Very interesting," said Clever.

They strolled across the tailored grassways towards the woods, with Clever remembering to ask about the two strange men in the doorway at the back of the room. Peter had seen them but didn't know who they were. He said he thought they looked like workmen, and he had been wondering about them as well. Clever kept up the questions, right until

Peter delivered them to the edge of the trees, firing one last query as he stepped into the shade under the leaves.

"And what about the red toetips?"

#

Peter was dreaming of being interrogated, strapped down on a table and blinded by a bright light.

His alarm clock buzzed at five in the morning, and he woke to find his bedclothes tangled around his body and his room light left on, having fallen asleep while reading the night before. He blinked at the alarm muzzily, and then remembered why he had set it so early. He stumbled out of bed, brushed his teeth, and stuck his head under the cold tap to wake himself up and to sort out his hair without having to use a comb. Not bothering with breakfast, he grabbed a handful of nuts as he swooped through the kitchen. Oops, nearly forgot, he thought. He backtracked to his bedroom and gently picked up the plane, tip-toed quietly back up the hallway, and then ruined his stealth efforts by banging out the screen door.

He squinted at the horizon, to where the sun was just making an appearance, colouring the sky with a mix of oranges, greys and light blues. It was going to be another glorious summer day and perfect for taking out the plane. Today was the day he had promised to take the Dinglemen flying. He just had to wait until all of the golfers were on their way and had played the first few holes, and then there would be some fairways free for the plane. Nobody else was playing on the course on tournament day, so it was perfect for the plane's first consumer flight. Peter couldn't help smiling at the idea. He couldn't wait until he had some spare time between the rush at the start of the tournament and when he would be needed again at the end of the day. A bit of a shortcut and a brisk march later, and he stashed the plane in the storage shed at the club and walked into the kitchen, ready for duty, suh!

It was a busy day. Peter spent the morning in a blur of orders. He wiped, carted, collected, cleaned, carried, greeted, delivered – and dreamed of his escape to test the plane with a passenger in it.

"Stop slacking off," said Caitlin at one

point, shoving past him with her hands full, "or go stand over in the corner where I don't have to keep walking around you."

Finally, the milling crowds emptied from the clubrooms. The tournament entrants were off on their rounds and the remaining spectators moved out to the tables on the balcony. Caitlin came back into the kitchen from delivering a platter to the dining area and told Peter she was fine to look after things until later. He didn't need telling twice. He had told the Dinglemen he would meet them at the end of fairway one, and he guessed they would be waiting for him by now.

#

Carrying the plane under an arm, he made a beeline down the middle of the fairway while enjoying the warmth of the sun on his face. When he neared the agreed meeting place he couldn't see the Dinglemen, but he could hear the raised voices of Clever and Sarge discussing who would get to go up in the plane first. He stopped and put the plane down, and it wasn't long before they stepped out from under some bushes alongside the fairway and scurried across to meet him. Clever and Sarge were still focused on being the first to fly and kept up their bickering. Weebit was watching them argue, but Nimin took one calculating look at the plane, glanced back at the others, turned to Peter and pointed a finger at himself. Peter nodded okay and Nimin climbed onto the wing, inched along the black line and flopped untidily into the front seat. Clever and Sarge only stopped their arguing, realising where Nimin was, when the propeller spun and the engine growled into action. He waved at them as the plane turned past where they stood gaping, mouthing something that looked like 'sucklers'. The engine growled once more, and then the plane, and its first ever live passenger, sped along the fairway.

"I'm going to kill him," said Sarge.

Clever just looked disgruntled, then shrugged at Sarge and turned to gawp at the speeding plane as it lifted off the ground and rocketed into the sky. Peter checked his watch to time the battery life and then asked the model plane to sweep up towards the tree tops, brush over the top leaves, then dip into the airspace above the next fairway. He wanted to make sure the plane didn't go across too far, to where the golfers were playing, but close enough Nimin would be able to see a good part of the golf course. The three Dinglemen at his feet were speechless, six pairs of boggling eyes trained on the little humming speck in the sky, and amazingly, carrying one of them within it. They would get a very good idea of the size of the golf course protecting their new home, Peter thought. He would suggest that next time, they take the model plane out on the back fairways to get a view over the woods and river and across to the buildings of the city. For now, he concentrated on making the plane glide along the trees between the two nearest fairways so Nimin could gaze out at the surrounding view and down onto the expanses of grass below.

Peter asked the plane to turn well before it flew past the clubrooms, and it was humming a return journey when he saw a small figure take the front steps of the club in a big leap and race towards where he was standing with the Dinglemen. Another figure shot down the stairs, then another and another. Peter had to keep most of his attention on the plane, but from where he stood it looked as if the small group were in pursuit of the first figure. As they drew closer, he saw the person at the front had a baseball cap pulled forward, obscuring Peter's view of his or her face. The person was being chased by some of the club members – Peter could see Caitlin and Daisy with them – and they were all getting farther and farther behind. The frontrunner veered away from where Peter was standing and headed towards a small gate in the fence at the end of fairway one. There was no way the group would catch them before they slipped through the gate and escaped. Peter glanced back into the sky. The plane was motoring back along the fairway, well above the heads of the running group.

"Stop him! He's got the prize money!"

"He's getting away!"

Peter was no closer than the others to the boy who, apparently realising he was so close to getting away, seemed to have found an extra fragment of speed. Without thinking about what he was doing Peter jerked the controls. The plane instantly replied by swerving after the running figure. It sped over the ground as it gave chase, diving down behind the whirling heels of the runaway. Well before it found its target, Peter cut the power. The plane looked as if it had a mind of its own as it did one final buck, twisted to the side, and crashed lengthwise into the back of the fleeing thief. He face-planted into the turf and the plane flipped over the top of his head and skidded to a halt several metres away. There was silence. It felt to Peter as if time paused for several seconds, the crowd moving in slow motion. The thief groaned, and it was only then that Peter remembered Nimin and felt a huge spurt of panic. Oh no!

Peter raced over, "Are you all right?"

"No!" squeaked the boy, pushing up from the ground.

"Not you!"

The crowd of chasing people grabbed the thief as Peter checked the plane, his back to the group. The passenger was wobbling slightly but was upright and had a huge smile on his face, shaking thumbs both pointing skyward. His rounded eyes were gleaming. "Can we do that again? Man, that was so maximal. Weeeeee!"

"Phew." Peter felt a gush of relief and blew

out a breath between pursed lips.

"Peter, are you apologising to your model plane?" asked Daisy.

Peter couldn't help himself – he checked the plane for damage. The left wing was partially torn from the body, the front of the right wing was crushed and grass-stained, and the silver prop needed repairing, but it didn't matter. He was lucky Nimin was fine and the Dinglemen were so forgiving of rough treatment. Actually, no, he was lucky the Dinglemen were all bonkers!

Peter turned back to where the crowd was surrounding the thief. Two of the golfers gripped an upper arm each, restraining the boy while they helped him to his feet. The boy was as short as Daisy, although plump, and was gabbling in a high pitched complaint at being hit by the plane.

One of the club members pulled an envelope out from under the thief's shirt and opened it to confirm it contained the prize money. Their hood was pushed back and some in the crowd gasped.

"Camilla!" one of members said. "You are going to be in a lot of trouble with your father!"

Camilla was frog-marched back to the clubrooms, with the whole crowd buzzing as they moved off, Caitlin, Daisy and Peter lagging behind.

"Do you know who that is?" Caitlin asked Peter.

"No, who?"

"The manager's daughter. And you just flattened her." She grinned at him before walking off.

"Oh, great." Peter muttered.

Daisy grimaced and then raised an eyebrow at him.

"I'm coming. I'll just be a few minutes."

As soon as she had walked after the crowd, Sarge, Clever and Weebit materialised next to Peter.

"My turn next," declared Sarge, narrowing his eyes at Clever to prevent discussion.

"The flying part looks spectacular. Surely, though, there is a better option for ground return," said Clever.

Peter wasn't quite sure how to reply. He was still recovering from his panic attack about Nimin and his responding smile felt a bit on the shaky side. He organised to meet up with the Dinglemen later and gathered up the plane, being careful with the torn wing, and then turned to head up the fairway to the clubrooms to see what would happen with Camilla. As he walked off with his damaged plane, he could hear Nimin yapping to the others in an awestruck voice.

"Wohooo, that was a ride. You have to try it. *Yehaa*! I'm all shaking. Look at me, Clever. I'm shaking. Wow. I want to do that again. You have to try it. That was a ride. Wooo weee—"

#

It had been agreed by everyone that no more would be said about thefts if Camilla was never seen at the club again, and Peter had been told that his plane wasn't welcome back either.

The last of the straggling golfers had finally completed their rounds, probably by cheating, thought Peter, switching golf balls or kicking them out of the rough when the other players weren't looking. He had heard one group fell so far behind they ducked between the bushes separating the green of fairway twelve from the tee-off area of fairway fourteen, thereby eliminating an entire pesky fairway. The club manager, Mr Smythe, was standing impatiently at the mike, tapping a polished dress shoe while happy golfers swayed and giggled back to their seats, apologising loudly as they bumped into or leaned on top of those already seated. He tapped the mike with an index finger and it whined in protest.

"Okay everybody, let's get on with the speeches," he boomed. "Hey you, quiet!" This was directed at a golfer near the front who was still giggling. The trophies were given out to clapping, and just as much booing and hooting, the retrieved prize money was eventually thrust into the hands of the three beaming winners, and then the manager held up a hand to quieten the crowd.

"I have one final piece of good news that the Board and I wish to share. We have been offered an opportunity that will ensure the future of this club." He stayed officiously silent until the room was hushed and every face looking in his direction. "As most of you will already know, we have been approached by financial backers to build a hotel and resort, to be attached to the golf club, and the committee has voted in favour." He smiled in the direction of the table near the front of the room, where the Board members were nodding and smiling. "This will bring in some much needed funding, allow us to upgrade the course, and attract new players. It will ensure that this golf course continues to be an asset to the city of Breadalbone."

Peter was standing in his usual spot at the back of the room. Most of the golfers wouldn't want new people at the club, he thought. They would be shown up too much. He smirked, thinking that, in fact, most would be shown up by a three year old with plastic clubs and a tennis ball. Apart from the odd urgent whispering to their direct neighbours the members seemed to be okay with the idea and Peter didn't really care either way. He didn't see how a resort, or hotel or whatever, would affect him in any way. Probably just more work, he thought. He guessed that was why the workmen had been there the previous day. One of the members asked how disruptive it would be while the resort was being built. Just where was it going to fit onto the golf course? No, the manager answered, it would not disrupt the club at all. The resort was going to be built on the other side of the golf course, in the woods.

Peter's head snapped up. What!? His mind raced as he listened to the questions from the assembled golfers. Most of them seemed to support the idea, although he got the feeling that none expected anything to happen for a long time, if at all. Surely they were right and he could relax and not panic straight away. Surely, to get the plans and permits and whatever was needed to build a big resort, would take months or even years. The more he listened, the more he relaxed. Financial backers pulled out of projects all of the time, didn't they? Besides, really, why would anyone put money into the Breadalbone golf club? Yeah, it'd be okay, he told himself. The manager boomed into the mike again, in answer to another question from the floor.

"We already have the necessary approvals. Clearing of the woods starts in ten days."

What!!?

CHAPTER EIGHT

That night, Peter tossed and turned, twisting his bed sheets into bunches. Mr Smythe and the Board were going to build in the woods! How many trees would have to go? What were the chances that this would happen *now*? More importantly, how was he going to tell the Dinglemen? They had trusted him when he said they would be safe in the woods. How was he to know? Those woods had been there for at least a hundred years. Longer. He sighed loudly and flipped over again.

Very early the next morning, he was out the door and on his way to see the Dinglemen. He wasn't looking forward to this meeting and he still hadn't worked out what he was going to say. As he got closer to the edge of the woods, his feet began to drag, his palms got sweaty and he felt a small hammering beginning behind his left eye. He really wished he didn't have to be the bearer of this piece of news.

They took it surprisingly well. Sarge kicked the tree nearest to him, showering them all with leaves and twigs, Nimin burst into tears, Weebit's jaw dropped and he looked towards their home, back to Peter, back to the woods, back to Peter, back to the woods, back to Peter, looking more and more hurt as his head pivoted. They left the accusations to Clever.

"But you said these woods were safe! You *said* we could live here! You said–"

Peter cut him off, his hands held out and his head hung low. "I know, I know. I'm sorry. These trees have been here forever. For generations! I just never thought that they wouldn't be here. And now Mr Smythe and his developers are going to ruin *everything*!" He slumped against the trunk of a tree and sat with his head in his hands.

"I'm so sorry. I've let you all down." He sniffed. There was silence and then Sarge spoke.

"Fine, it's not your fault," he grunted, surprising everyone that he had let Peter off the hook first.

Clever sighed. "What are the chances this building won't go ahead?" he asked.

"I don't know, but it doesn't sound likely."

"Will they tear down everything?"

"I don't know."

Nimin pleaded to Peter, "But Weebit's making us a really great home. It's even got a lookout already and a balcony and a cooking pit just for me and sleeping chambers and we even slept in the lookout and we could see stars and Weebit's worked so hard and I don't want to go!" He burst into tears again.

"Enough, Nimin," Sarge put a soothing hand on his arm. He turned to Clever. "Perhaps you just need time to think. We need to come up with a way to stop this resort building from happening."

Peter just felt more miserable, but Weebit and Nimin suddenly brightened and appeared to trust that Clever would be able to fix everything.

"We've chosen here," continued Sarge bitterly. "I will not let humans move us along." He glared at Peter.

Clever cleared his throat and looked thoughtful. He pursed his lips, sat on a tree root and stared at the tree in front of him.

"I'm really—" Peter began.

"Shssshh," said Sarge, not taking his eyes off Clever. Clever shook his head.

"Peter, we'll need your help," said Clever. "We are going to have to slow down the clearing of the woods. We need to create time so we can devise a plan to save Dingledell."

"Anything. I'll do anything I can."

"We are not going to let go of our new home. Not easily, not now." Clever set his jaw.

"We'll show them." Sarge shadow boxed with the tree he had kicked.

"Yeah," Nimin smiled at Weebit and blinked away a few remaining tears.

\#

The morning the work was to start saw Clever and the others peering around the last of the trees at the end of the woods, their eyes peeled for movement beyond the black fence. Glancing to the side, Clever could see Peter skulking nearby on the golf course, pretending to collect golf balls while also watching for signs of arrival of the workmen. Peter had thought that this was the most likely access site to bring in the equipment for tearing up the woods. So here is where they would wait.

The Dinglemen had just settled themselves behind the largest tree, the fifth in from the golf course, when they heard the grumble of a large truck. It was still early and they hadn't had to wait long. Clever felt Peter crouch on the pine needles behind them but didn't turn to acknowledge his arrival. He was too busy ogling at the size of the truck as it rolled into view. The truck was so large it didn't even bother to move off the road. It just loudly hissed to a stop in the middle, holding up the motorcars that were jammed up behind it in an impatient tail. Clever couldn't help staring at the number of wheels spread unevenly along the length, from the narrow windowed part at the front to the very back of the long tray behind it. His eyes travelled up from the wheels, drawn by the bright yellow of the monster that was riding on top of the truck. It was a squat, mean-looking, yellow and black machine with belts instead of tyres, a vicious claw facing the back and a large scraper at the front, and only a small enclosed window space for a human. He had seen similar machines before, even the same colour, but none so intimidating, and never so close.

"What is that?" he hissed.

"A bulldozer," Peter hissed back.

A human leapt down from the front of the truck and strutted down the side of the tray towards the rear. Another human was walking down the other side of the truck, given away by a pair of legs that could be seen whenever there was a break between the huge black tyres. They met up at the back, where they fussed with two separated silver metal ramps. Once they had them lowered, one human jumped up onto the tray, clambered into the bulldozer, and seconds later it roared to life. And it was *loud*. Clever watched it lumber down the ramps, taking note of the size of the concave scraper it carried. He winced, looked along the row of trees, looked back at the scraper, and thought that if he believed in the gods he would probably start praying to them about now. If there were any more of these bulldozer machines arriving, the woods, and Dingledell with them, would be flattened in a matter of a few short days. The humans climbed back into the truck, it grumbled alive, whooshed air and trundled off, leading away its parade of frustrated motorcars. The bulldozer was left to squat menacingly on the outside of the fence. As the last of the motorcars crawled past their spot, another motorcar, a type of motorcar-truck, came barrelling along the road towards them. Clever glanced at Peter again.

"That's called a Holden Jackaroo."

To Clever, the Hold-On Jackaroo looked to be going way too fast. Metal complained as it swerved and hit the concrete of the ditch, the two passengers bouncing wildly inside, before the Hold-On skidded to a stop near the bulldozer. Two rusty, mismatched doors squealed open and two workmen climbed out. Clever didn't look at them immediately, though. His attention had been caught by a stuffed toy rabbit, roped spread-eagled onto a set of silver bars attached to the front of the Hold-On. He made a mental note to ask Peter about it. Were they hunters? The ageing Hold-On had two large round lights attached to the roof, presumably to help with the hunt? And how difficult would it be to catch a stuffed rabbit? Even Nimin was perfectly capable of catching a real one.

When Clever turned his attention to the

humans, he was only half surprised to realise he recognised them. It was the two workmen he had seen when they joined the humans for luncheon – the tree trunk and the twig. They collected boxes out of the back of the Hold-On and strolled towards the fence, where they dumped their small loads and strolled back. They didn't appear to be in any hurry to start work, and were making a second dawdling progression with half-laden arms when the fat man roared up in another, newer looking motorcar-truck. This time, Clever didn't even need to glance at Peter.

"Mercedes, a four-wheel drive. Expensive."

Clever didn't know what these names were supposed to mean, but he nodded anyway. The fat man leapt down, appeared to chatter at the workmen for a few minutes while they nodded, then he climbed back into the motorcar-truck and roared off. Whatever he had said made the workmen move a lot faster. Clever hoped he would be able to hear what they were saying to each other, and he smiled thinly when their voices carried through the fence as they squared up to cut the nearest section.

"Dammit Durdle, get out of my way."

"Sure Boggs."

"Cut that end. Not like that, idiot. No, don't cut that. I said, stop!"

A taut fence wire pinged between the large cutters gripped by the one called Durdle. The wire whipped back, narrowly missing the other workman's head, and cracked loudly against the front of the Hold-On. The big workman, the one called Boggs, swore loudly at Durdle, the twig, and turned away to inspect the damage to the motorcar. His back stiffened and he looked to be taking a lot of deep breaths to calm down. He hadn't turned back.

"Sorry about that Boggs, my mistake."

Boggs turned slowly, deliberately. His face was a dark purple and in a bunched fist he gripped the halved remains of the stuffed toy.

"I said sorry." Durdle gazed coolly at Boggs while he ranted.

Clever couldn't understand any of the words that Boggs yelled. He nudged Peter and squinted up at him.

"What language is that?"

Boggs took a long time to calm down. He nagged and bullied Durdle, who just ignored him, while they worked at peeling back a section of the fence to allow access for the bulldozer. Both workmen were wearing the same clothes as before, the same bright vests over short-sleeved khaki tunics, black shorts and heavy boots. Now that Clever had a chance to look at them properly, he saw that Boggs had grease stains on his tunic and splatters of paint on his shorts, while Durdle looked as if his clothes were new and without a single wrinkle. Clever nodded approval. Durdle had also tried to paste his hair into place, but it flicked off his forehead to reveal angry red spots to match those on his chin. With his protuberant eyes, long limbs and deliberate manner, he gave Clever the impression of being less like a twig and more like a praying mantis. The only clothing he wore that looked out of place to Clever were green and white striped socks, yanked right up to wonky looking kneecaps. Clever turned his attention back to Boggs. He looked older than Durdle, maybe in his fourth decade, although Clever wasn't sure, and he looked mean. He had a jutting square jaw and his nose was squashed across his face beneath piggy black eyes and bushy black eyebrows. Clever deduced the Hold-On, and the remnants of the stuffed rabbit, belonged to Boggs.

Another large truck, although nowhere near the size of the first, rolled up the road just as Durdle worked to roll the fence wire back tidily to one side. Boggs left him to it and walked out to the road to direct the truck through the gap in the fence. It reversed big rear wheels, layering a tread pattern on the short grass, and hardly noticed the concrete ditch as it backed and angled through the gap. Clever could see that a large rectangular container and a small upright box were both catching a ride on the back. Peter whispered what he thought they were as each was swung down to the ground.

"I'm guessing that's a portable office," he said. "Maybe they'll keep plans and stuff in there. It might be some help to us."

The smaller item was swung down.

"And that's a port-a-loo, so the workmen will have somewhere to, you know, *go*."

"Ewww."

Boggs signed a bit of paper for the driver of the truck, and with a cool wave from Durdle, it rolled back out onto the road and left. Everything was quiet again, until Boggs started up the bulldozer. Clever looked at the others in dismay, seeing the same emotion reflected back on each face. They had thought it would take most of the day for the workmen to get set up, and here they were, ready to go, already. He was crushed. Their Dingledell, and his balcony, were going to be destroyed in no time. The bulldozer roared again, swung forward, and growled towards the line of trees.

The Dinglemen and Peter scrambled backward and fled. Clever leapt over tree roots as he raced with the others, his heart pounding as he listened for the terrible sounds to begin. He imagined he could already hear the cracking as the first tree gave way to the onslaught. The Dinglemen were already well into the woods, Peter not far behind them, when the noise of the bulldozer died. Clever exchanged glances with the others and they slunk back towards their tree to see what was going on. Boggs was climbing down from the bulldozer. Leaving the entry swung open, he walked back towards the portable office.

"Smoko!"

Clever looked at Peter.

"Morning tea break."

"Why are you stopping now? And you've left the cab open," said Durdle.

"Because, Durdle, I stop when I want to. And the cabin stinks of stale smoke. You can keep working if you want but I'm taking my break."

Boggs pulled some metal steps out of the portable office, placed them at the door and went in. Durdle shrugged, walked out to the back of the Hold-On and returned with a basket. Boggs backed out of the office carrying two flattened chairs. He threw one down for Durdle, adjusted his own and sank into it with a loud creak. His face twisted with disdain when he noticed the basket Durdle put down between their chairs. Clever thought it was pretty, with pink and white gingham trim and a lace border around the top. Durdle was still setting up his chair.

"So, did mummy remember to pack in paper umbrellas?" asked Boggs in a syrupy voice.

Durdle turned, a sardonic smile on his face. "My mother loves me. What can I say? I'll ask for umbrellas for tomorrow, shall I?"

Boggs glared at him, and Durdle returned his gaze with a cool stare.

Clever looked across at the bulldozer, wondering again how long their trees would last against a monster like that. He cocked his head to the side as he considered the bulldozer.

"Peter, does that thing need a key?" he whispered.

"I'm pretty sure it does. Why?" Peter hissed back.

"The human didn't have the key on him."

Five heads swivelled towards the bulldozer.

"No, I think workmen tend to leave the keys in the ignition. Oh, good point."

Sarge nudged Clever in the side with an elbow, grinned briefly, and sidled away to make a beeline towards the bulldozer and the keys.

"I'll even share my sandwiches. Do you want ham and cheese or corned beef and pickle?" asked Durdle, his hands fossicking around inside the basket.

Sarge bulleted along the trees, then with a quick check in the direction of the workmen, he sped across to the bulldozer, made short work of scaling the metal crawling-belt, and entered the inside of the machine.

"Beef."

An instant later the keys appeared at the entry, and Clever held his breath as he watched Sarge leap down onto the metal crawling-belt with them clutched firmly to his chest. Clever winced at the thought of the keys hitting the yellow metal. Sarge was a silver blur as he hit the grass and raced back to the others, the keys gripped under an arm. He skidded into place and was standing beside Clever again before Durdle could hand Boggs his sandwich. Sarge smirked and gave the keys to Peter to put into his pocket.

"Well done," Peter hissed, "and good thinking, Clever."

Clever preened. At that moment, Nimin, who had been watching the food, squeaked excitedly. His eyes were locked on something tiny and red that fluttered down from behind Durdle. Something Durdle had been hiding from Boggs by tucking it at the back of his chair. Nimin was off like a shot, before either he or Sarge could grab him. Clever frowned as he watched Nimin dash across the grass, skid beneath the chair, grab the red object, and speed back to where they stood in the woods.

Peter raised his eyebrows, and Sarge and Clever, and even Weebit, scowled at Nimin, but he looked too pleased with himself to care that he might be in trouble. He held his prize proudly in his arms. Clever looked at it for a few seconds before he worked out what it was. A red paper umbrella.

#

Peter was shocked that neither Boggs nor Durdle had even looked up from their sandwiches.

"Jeez, people really don't see a thing," he muttered. He couldn't get over how easily the Dinglemen had helped themselves to the keys and umbrella. He glanced at Clever, thinking maybe this explained a lot of life's little mysteries, and made a note to ask if the Dinglemen had a thing about collecting odd socks.

Shaking his head, he turned back to watch the workmen. Boggs finished his sandwich, and leaving his chair where it was, he stretched and sauntered back over to the bulldozer.

The workmen turned everything up-side

down looking for the keys, Peter and the Dinglemen listening as Boggs's swearing became more and more colourful. He even dumped out the contents of the picnic basket, scattering food, plastic plates, cutlery and napkins onto the grass between the chairs, and only hissed at the little packet of umbrellas. A calm Durdle looked under the chairs, in the Jackaroo, walked across to check in the cabin of the bulldozer for the third time, and again came up empty. After twenty minutes of solid searching, he shrugged his shoulders and stared at Boggs. Boggs glared and growled at Durdle to stay put while he went to get spare keys. He climbed into the Jackaroo, bounced back across the ditch and fishtailed down the road, leaving Durdle to methodically tidy the spilled contents of the basket. Once he had finished, and the basket carefully stowed inside the portable office, he glanced around with a bored expression and sat back down in his chair.

"This is perfect. Guys, I think it's time for Durdle to have a little nap," said Peter. He pulled his basket closer and started to take the golf balls from off the top, revealing a large and slightly dented cellophane-wrapped slice of chocolate cake hidden on the bottom. He took out the cake, pushed the balls back in and picked up both cake and basket, and then looked up into Nimin's accusing eyes.

"Sorry, Nimin, but this cake is spiked with something to help him sleep. I promise, I'll make it up to you."

Peter crouched while he moved along the trees, checked the coast was clear and stepped out onto the bottom fairway, where he started whistling and swinging the basket as he walked around towards the worksite.

"Hello? Anyone here?"

Durdle's head poked around the side of the portable office.

"Hi," Peter called, "I've been sent with some morning tea from the kitchen." As he walked around the corner, he feigned surprise.

"Is it just you working here—?" He paused to let Durdle introduce himself.

"Bruce—everyone calls me Durdle."

"Peter. I work at the club." They shook hands.

"No, my workmate has just gone to get— some supplies," Durdle finished lamely.

"More cake for you then, I won't tell." Peter grinned. Durdle smiled back as he accepted the cake, and Peter guessed that Durdle would eat it all, despite the sandwiches he had just eaten. They seemed to have a similar build, and he was always hungry. Durdle waved him to Boggs's chair and sat to unwrap the slice. Peter sat and made small talk for a few minutes while Durdle ate and then started to yawn.

"Do you have any idea how long it will take to clear these woods?" Peter asked.

"Dunno, maybe a few days, three at most," Durdle answered around a mouthful. He yawned again, giving Peter an eyeful of chocolate sludge and tonsils.

"Not long then." He had known it wouldn't take long, but Peter couldn't help but feel disappointed.

"Nah, we're working fast on this job."

Peter sat forward, but tried not to sound too interested. "Really? Why?"

Durdle seemed happy to share with his new friend. He tapped his nose with a long bony finger. "Well, it sounds as if someone is anxious to have their resort built, pronto." He yawned again.

"You mean Mr Smythe, the club manager?"

"Nah, not him. He's not the boss." Durdle

closed his eyes and slumped a bit lower in his chair.

"He's not? Then who is?"

Durdle mumbled. "Not very nice men—" His voice trailed off into deep breathing. His hand fell beside the chair, letting the chocolate-smeared wrapper land in the grass near his feet, a blur flashing from the woods causing Peter to dive for the ground. He just managed to scoop the wrapper up in time, winking at an aggrieved Nimin who had launched himself at it milliseconds too late. Both of them panicked when Durdle snorted in his sleep.

Peter checked Durdle again to make sure he was sleeping solidly, and then smiling to himself he walked over to check the door on the portable office, the smile widening when he saw the standard lock, the keys swinging in place. For a brief moment he stood undecided on the steps, but he doubted he would have time to search inside, and he didn't want to get caught by Boggs. He did think he had time to turn the lock around. Completing the job quickly, he pushed in the locking button, which was now facing the outside, and gently closed the door until it was just sitting against the door-jamb. He added the office keys to the others in his pocket, along with the cake wrapper, and checked that he had left nothing behind. He had just finished telling Nimin what he wanted him to do, and scrunched himself back under the shade of the trees, when he heard an engine revving loudly as it grew closer. The Jackaroo leapt the ditch again and left deep skid marks in the grass as it jerked to stop beside the office.

Boggs looked livid when he saw Durdle happily snoozing away the morning. He marched over and tried to wake Durdle by raising a solid workboot and kicking over his chair. Both fell sideways, the chair still partially cradling Durdle, who just mumbled in his sleep and snuggled into the grass. Peter gasped when Boggs stomped back towards the Jackaroo. He wasn't going to run him over, was he? Fortunately, Boggs continued around to the back of the vehicle and returned with a large white container. He turned the container upside-down and dumped water all over Durdle's head and body. Durdle snorted awake, took one muzzy look at Boggs standing over him, and struggled to get out of the chair and off the ground, eventually managing to thrust the chair away. It took him a few tries to get his legs to obey orders, but soon he was standing on his feet and dripping water onto the surrounding grass.

"I must have nodded off," said Durdle, sounding as though he didn't particularly care that Boggs looked set to explode. Peter thought Durdle would get a right drubbing and he was right. Boggs yelled at Durdle while he stood dripping, Boggs kept yelling when a tapping noise came from inside the office, and Boggs was still swearing when they both went to investigate the sound, each climbing the short flight of stairs and stepping inside. His voice was only cut off when he slammed the door behind them to reiterate his point. Gotcha, thought Peter. All was quiet for a minute, with plenty of time for Nimin to get back to the others and give Peter an expectant grin.

"Well done, Nimin."

A bellow erupted from within the office. The flimsy walls shuddered as someone, probably Boggs, tried to kick the door open, and then the whole office rocked wildly with the sound of stomping boots, thumps and crashes. Peter and the Dinglemen exchanged smiles as the yells from the office got louder and more desperate. It seemed like ages had passed before both workmen finally grew hoarse and fell quiet. Hopefully, prayed Peter, nobody would let them out until the end of the day because he had to go and collect some golf balls.

CHAPTER NINE

It was well after seven that night, and Peter and the Dinglemen were back to surveillance from behind the fifth tree, with a supply of food scrounged from his parents' kitchen – a tuna sandwich, a handful of chocolate biscuits and a packet of doughnuts. The evening was still light and Peter didn't want to risk being seen near the worksite, but they all wanted to know if anyone was going to come by and release the workmen from inside the office. They had been back in their spot long enough to be bored by the wait, and Peter was telling the Dinglemen shortened versions of stories he could remember from his childhood and the Dinglemen were sitting around him using the doughnuts as comfy seats. Except for Weebit, who had his doughnut around his waist like a tutu. Nimin's chair had a distinct sagging look and he was still plucking small handfuls of dough, sugar and cinnamon from around his legs and licking his fingers as he listened to Peter tell the stories. He was halfway through a rather creative version of a pirate story when the Dinglemen stiffened and cocked their heads, Clever holding up a hand. Then Peter could hear it, too. The sound of a vehicle slowing as it neared the worksite.

Peter twisted around and leaned forward to see around the tree trunk, spying Mr Smythe as he drove through the opening in the fence to park beside the Jackaroo. The workmen had also heard him arrive, because they resumed their yelling and banging against the walls of the office. The look on Mr Smythe's face through the windscreen was comical, as he took in the fact that all of the trees were still standing and the workmen must have been locked inside the office for the entire day. He stormed across to fling open the door and was shoved aside by Durdle, who made a desperate line for the port-a-loo, followed immediately out the door by Boggs, who relieved himself against the side of the office, his back to the woods. Mr Smythe inspected the reversed door lock, frowned and pursed his lips, and then turned to stare with narrowed eyes at the grounds and then at the woods. His gaze swept along the bottom of the trees and stopped when he was looking straight at the fifth tree in from the fairway. He peered directly at where Peter was crouched. Peter froze, horrified, sure that Mr Smythe could see him, and he only started breathing again when Mr Smythe eventually looked away, gesturing for Boggs and Durdle to follow him.

He led them behind the back of the Mercedes, so that from behind the tree Peter could only hear bits and pieces of what was being said. A few loud words carried and he knew the workmen were in deep trouble for getting locked in the office. He felt a bit sorry for Durdle but not for Boggs. Mr Smythe slammed the back of the four-wheel-drive and stalked back towards the office with the workmen in tow, Durdle carrying a cardboard box that he stashed inside the office before returning to stand stone-faced in front of Mr Smythe. Mr Smythe glared at them again and spoke loudly enough for Peter to hear him say something about a deadline. His voice rose as he got more agitated.

"—better have this ground cleared on target. You know they won't accept excuses, and I will not be blamed! Do you understand me?"

He sounded angry, as Peter would have expected. But there was something else in Mr Smythe's voice, something that Peter had a hard time connecting with him. He also sounded worried. Very worried. Clever prodded Peter's ankle to get his attention and shrugged in enquiry. Peter shook his head. He wondered again who *they* were, remembering Durdle's comment about them. *Not nice men.* He thought that he and the Dinglemen should check in the office as soon as possible. Maybe something in the office would tell them about the investors, and besides, he wanted to know what was in the cardboard box that Mr Smythe had delivered.

They only had to wait for another few minutes for Mr Smythe to slam back into the Mercedes and career away, and not much longer after that before the workmen had clambered into the Jackaroo and followed him. Peter and the Dinglemen watched the rear lights until the vehicle turned out of sight before any of them felt comfortable speaking, and even then they spoke in hushed voices. The decision was made that it would be safest to search the office first thing in the morning, hours before the workmen were due to arrive. It wasn't likely that anyone would return that night but Peter didn't want to take the risk of getting caught. Agreeing to meet again before dawn, they headed their separate ways, Peter watching the Dinglemen melt away between the trees and then walking towards the clubrooms and home.

It was still dark when Clever stepped out of Dingledell and squinted around with red-rimmed eyes at the shapes of the surrounding trees. Sarge energetically pushed past him, increasing his desire to return to bed. At least he could hear that Nimin was still grumbling well inside the cavern. When Weebit silently stepped around him to follow after Sarge, Clever suppressed a sigh and called for Nimin to quit complaining and get moving. By the time they met up with Peter at the worksite the sky was just starting to lighten to a grey, tinged with pink and orange.

The fat man and the workmen hadn't bothered to fix the lock the evening before, which didn't bode well for anything of value being kept in the portable office. Clever had agreed with the others, however, that it would be remiss of them not to search inside. Peter opened the door of the office and they crept in to search. Only when they were all standing inside the door and it had been pulled closed, a piece of cardboard preventing them from being locked in, did Peter turn on his torch. He swung the beam of light slowly across the few pieces of furniture within, while Clever screwed up his nose at the dank odour of stale human sweat and unwashed garments. Pheeurgh.

"Let's search and leave as quickly as possible," he said.

"Maybe we should leave the door open?" suggested Peter.

They moved forward to look around, leaving Nimin and Weebit near the door to act as sentries and warn them if they heard anything outside. In the torch light, Clever could see that the office contained a small table in the corner to the left of the door, four of those flattened folding chairs leaning against the opposite wall, and a flimsy looking desk just ahead of where he stood. In the corner behind the desk sat a small cabinet of drawers, the cardboard box sitting on top of it. Peter headed straight for the cabinet, while Sarge and Clever scaled a desk leg to stand on the desktop. They watched Peter as he placed the torch down on the desk and turned towards the box on the cabinet, casting a long, twisted shadow onto the office wall. Lifting the box down, he opened the top and peered in.

"Geez, it's just toilet paper. It's not exactly the incriminating evidence that we need."

"Oh. Let's see what's in the cabinet," directed Clever.

Peter tried each drawer of the cabinet in turn, starting from the top. They were all locked. He turned back to grimace at Sarge and Clever, pursed his lips, then tried a set of keys he pulled from his pocket – the small set he had collected when he turned around the lock on the door the previous evening. The last key that he tested worked. Quickly, he slid out the top drawer, found it empty, opened the next down and rifled through the few papers within. He placed a few pages and letters on the desk for Clever to read, and with Sarge breathing down his neck Clever walked across the papers, looking for anything of interest. He didn't see any names other than the fat man's and the contents appeared to be innocent items, such as the quote for hiring the office and some basic drawings of the area. Very little was being kept in the cabinet and they were done in minutes, Clever shaking his head when he was finished with the papers.

"Nothing of use to us here," he said, disappointed.

He watched with a critical eye to confirm that Peter put the papers back where he had found them and that he relocked the cabinet.

"Pssst!" Nimin was gesturing from the doorway. Peter immediately flicked off the torch, throwing the office into near darkness. Sarge and Clever sped over to the door to join the others, while behind them Peter crept across the floor as softly as he could, making sure he didn't make any loud noise. They all huddled near the door, listening for the sounds that Nimin had heard alerting him to whatever, or whoever, was outside. And there it was. Clever could hear stealthy movements, a sort of brushing along the front of the portable office, moving towards the crack in the doorway where five pairs of ears were glued and five pairs of lungs held their breath.

Clever could feel his heart racing and wished he was somewhere else, in his bedding, preferably, or perhaps in his old laboratory. He peered at the others, imagining they all looked as concerned as he felt. Except for Sarge, of course, who was bound to be enjoying this. Clever heard a soft scrape against the door and was troubled by what would happen to Peter if he got caught. He turned worried eyes to look up at Peter's face but it was too gloomy to see his expression. Clever turned back to the door, mildly surprised when the scraping moved past and stealthy footsteps faded away in the direction of the woods.

They waited. A few minutes later, Clever thought he heard a metallic clang and a faint rasping noise. Sarge turned to look at him to see if he had heard it. He nodded, yes, he had heard, and then shook his head to say he didn't know what was going on out there. Sarge shrugged. He didn't know, either.

Whoever was out there, thought Clever, it wasn't safe for Peter to leave the office just yet. Clever was glad his nostrils could fit between the door and the door jamb, because the smell in the office hadn't improved any. As well as the pong of stale sweat, Nimin was nervous. He saw Sarge scowl at Nimin, who just shrugged an apology and jostled Clever so he could also press his nose to the fresh air. They listened in uncomfortable silence for several more minutes, and then Clever heard soft footfalls move back past the door and continue around the corner of the office. He felt Sarge and Nimin stiffen beside him and knew they could hear it, too. The human had moved off, and given the direction they went, it appeared they must have entered via the road, not the golf grounds. It could have been anyone.

Peter got their attention and indicated for Sarge to head out to see if the coast was clear. The other Dinglemen all slipped out with him, glad to be out of the stinky box. Sarge bolted around the side of the office in the direction of the footsteps, but shortly came back, shaking his head. He hadn't seen anyone. He tapped the bottom of the door and Peter opened it enough to slink out to join them, the group moving off to complete the second part of their planned mission before the workmen arrived for the day. Because of the human interloper, they had spent much longer in the office than intended and the morning had arrived. The grey sky had given way to a very light blue with a few wispy clouds on the horizon and, in the distance, a flock of tiny dark birds spiralled above the woods. Clever frowned at the birds, his mind worrying at why someone else would be sneaking around the worksite at dawn.

"Now the bulldozer," said Sarge, leading them towards it and rubbing his hands together. Peter had told them he would unlock the metal flap on the side of the bulldozer to give the Dinglemen access to the motor, while he would see what he could do from inside the cabin. Their job was going to be to use the small metal files Peter had brought along to cause as much damage as possible to the interior of the engine. Sarge had been looking forward to this all night, so as soon as they reached the bulldozer he led Clever and the others in scaling the huge metal crawling-bands. They skittered up onto the sides and balanced on a convenient handle, ready near the cover of the motor in anticipation of slicing hoses and wrecking parts. Peter lifted up the black cover and they all blinked in surprise, slowly lowering their weapons when they saw the state of the engine. It wasn't that there was no damage that could be done – it was that someone had beaten them to it. The motor was a mess. Any hose to be cut had been cut, often several times. Metal lines had been slashed through and had bled a pale fluid, and there were gaping holes where parts obviously belonged but had been removed.

"No, well, oh, dang boggit!" grumbled Sarge. He looked crushed. There was nothing left for them to do. They got themselves back down to the ground and moved around to the front of the bulldozer where, now that he was looking, Clever could see a shiny black fluid puddled underneath. The human had done the work for them and they had done the job well. Peter relocked the cover over the motor, and with a final check that nothing had been left behind, they headed back into the woods. Clever frowned as he walked, wondering about the human who had been so destructive to the bulldozer. Someone else obviously didn't want the woods torn down, but who were they and why?

#

Peter was sitting at the table in the club kitchen, carefully testing a cup of hot chocolate to see if it had cooled enough to drink. Seated across from him, Caitlin and Daisy had started their day, but it was still a bit too early for him to be out on the grounds without raising suspicion. A loud shout made him slurp his drink and burn his tongue. Hastily, he set the mug down and listened to what appeared to be Mr Smythe shouting at someone in his office. Peter guessed it was one of the hapless workmen, there to tell the bad news about the bulldozer. He and the girls exchanged glances while the ranting from down the hallway went on for several minutes, the other person presumably replying during the short periods of quiet between outbursts. Peter was beginning to think the yelling would never end. He tested his hot chocolate again. The office door must have been opened, just then, because the last thing Mr Smythe shouted was easily heard in the kitchen.

"—and go out the back way!"

It wasn't long before Boggs stomped past the kitchen door, red-faced and staring straight ahead, with his lips moving as if he was muttering under his breath. He looked furious and he swore loudly when he thought he was out of earshot of anyone in the club.

"I wonder what's going on?" said Daisy, looking intrigued.

"I don't know," said Caitlin, "but I do know one thing. I do not want to run into Mr Smythe today."

As Daisy nodded in response, more yelling could be heard from Mr Smythe's office. Daisy froze mid-nod and looked at Peter as if she expected he could tell her who was being yelled at now. He shrugged his shoulders and shook his head, he didn't know. But he intended to find out.

"I'd better be getting out to work," he said, standing and leaving his half-finished drink on the table. The girls waved vaguely as he backed out of the kitchen, their heads cocked to hear if more shouting would be forthcoming. Instead of going immediately out the back door, Peter crept quietly down the hallway past Mr Smythe's office and slowed his pace as he passed the door. He could just make out a furious hiss from inside.

"—writing to your head office over this, do you hear me? I will not wait a whole week for a replacement! What about from another city?"

Peter couldn't hear a reply. Then Mr Smythe spoke again.

"None. Not one available? I don't believe a word of it. How do you stay in business?" There was another silence.

"Not as sorry as you will be, I promise you that."

Peter heard the sound of a handset being slammed back into its cradle and took that as his cue to speed off down the hall. He didn't slow until he had leapt down the steps, jumped the nearest garden bed and rounded the corner. This would not be a good time to get caught loitering outside Mr Smythe's office. He had been on the phone to someone and he couldn't get a replacement. A replacement for what? Peter prayed it was the bulldozer, and he hoped Mr Smythe couldn't get hold of another any time soon. That would be very good news for us, he thought, although he wondered how long they could hold off what seemed to be inevitable. He really couldn't see how they were going to be able to stop the resort from going ahead.

CHAPTER TEN

The next morning, Peter threw back the covers and grumbled out of bed, absently patted the still-damaged plane, and sleepwalked down the narrow hall towards the bathroom. His mother was already up and working on her latest artwork, and she didn't seem aware of how early it was, just asking him if he would like to join her for breakfast before he left. They dined on cornflakes in a companionable silence before each returned to what they had been doing. These early starts were really becoming a rotten habit, Peter muzzily complained to his reflection while he brushed his teeth. The bulldozer had roared to life again late yesterday afternoon. He and the Dinglemen had exchanged disgusted looks, and between them could think of no better plan than to sabotage the bulldozer again, unless their fellow saboteur beat them to it for a second night. They had no choice but to slow down the felling of the trees any way they could and hope they would find out something about the owners or Mr Smythe that might stop the resort from going ahead. Peter spat out toothpaste foam. From the way Durdle spoke about the owners, there was a good chance something was dodgy about them. He just wished he knew what it was.

"Attractive," he muttered sarcastically at his image in the mirror, eyeing his dark-ringed, puffy eyes and unruly hair."

He turned away from the sink, still thinking about their plans. He and the Dinglemen had discussed breaking into Mr Smythe's office, and while he broke out into a cold sweat at the idea, it made sense. Any information about the investors, especially information they didn't want people to know, would most likely be locked away somewhere in that office. There just had to be something fishy about them, since they even seemed to have Mr Smythe scared and in a hurry to complete the work on time. And aside from that, if there wasn't anything dishonest about the investors the resort would go ahead, the Dinglemen would have to leave, and he just didn't want to think about that happening. Peter wondered again, why the tight deadline for getting the resort built? There had to be a reason. It was a thin straw to grasp at, he knew, but it was the only straw he had.

#

Some cloud cover meant that it was much darker than yesterday morning, and Peter followed the line of trees flanking the top fairway towards the clubrooms rather than turn on his torch. He knew that if he stayed close enough to the trees he would avoid falling in the bunker that was somewhere about halfway along the fairway. He paused when he was directly opposite from the clubrooms, peering across the dark ground at the pale white pools cast by the security lights spaced along the roofline, checking as he did so that all of the interior lights were off. The windows were darker rectangles against the walls of the building and all seemed to be quiet. The clubrooms looked alien at night, the outside tables and chairs tinged a glowing white as if they would electrocute anyone who tried to sit, the flowers in the garden an iridescent blue-white, oddly coloured by the security lights.

He turned away and stepped through the line of trees, then walked across the neighbouring fairway towards the woods. A sliver of moon just peeked through where the clouds were breaking up, allowing him to see darker shadows where the trees loomed against the night. He followed the outside of the woods and was at the meeting spot behind the fifth tree well before the Dinglemen arrived. He only knew they were with him when Sarge grunted at him.

"Are you coming, human?"

The Dinglemen all melted past him towards the worksite. Peter followed them and halted when the dark, squat bulk of the bulldozer suddenly appeared in front of him. He had nearly walked into it. He finally switched his torch on, keeping a hand over it to minimise the light given off, and ran the torch down the length of the machine. The bulldozer didn't look tampered with, but then they hadn't seen the damage yesterday, so he walked forward to unlock the cover over the motor.

And froze, when he heard the rattle of thick chains. Out of the corner of his eye he could see the black outline of a huge dog, a Rottweiler, as it stalked around the blade at the front of the bulldozer. Peter heard Nimin squeak, but he couldn't help swinging the torch at the dog to reveal bared razor teeth and raised hackles, all the more terrifying in the yellow beam of torch light. The dog reacted to the light by snarling in outrage and launching towards the source. Adrenalin surging, Peter threw the torch, arcing it towards the back of the bulldozer and praying the dog would chase after the light beam. The Rottweiler twisted mid-stride to follow, then pulled up short, shook a pendulous head and turned its malevolent attention back to Peter. The torch landed facing back towards him, making him feel even more exposed. He felt glued to the spot, his heart leaping into his throat. With no hope of climbing onto the bulldozer before the dog cut him off, he could only run and pray the dog ran out of chain before it caught him. He whirled on his heel and sprinted. Over the sound of his own racing feet and the blood rushing in his ears, he heard the rumble of the chain as the dog launched in pursuit, and then a loud swishing as the chain tore through the grass behind him. Within seconds, he could feel the ground behind him pulse with the dog's pounding stride and feel the heat from its breath on his legs.

"Wooee! Doggie Ahoy!" whooped Sarge.

The dog growled in rage, the heat was instantly gone and the only pounding was in his chest, but Peter didn't dare stop running so he half twisted to look over a shoulder. Then stopped and gaped in surprise and horror. In the gloom cast from the torch, he could make out Sarge *standing* on top of the dog's head, gripping an ear in each outstretched hand and riding the movement like a cross between a rodeo cowboy and a big wave surfer. The dog had completely forgotten about Peter and was wildly throwing its head around to remove Sarge. If it was successful, Sarge would be eaten, there was no doubt about it. The dog bucked and twisted, shook its head violently and then sprinted off around the bulldozer, growling viciously as it shook and tossed. Peter raced over to grab the torch, trying to follow the crazed dog, trying to keep an eye on Sarge, and maybe, if he could, help distract the dog. It stopped dead, tested shaking again, even rolling and scraping its ears on the ground to remove the tiny irritant riding on its head. In the light from the torch, Peter could see the dog's eyes rolling and spittle flying from its mouth.

"Yee-ha!" Sarge was enjoying himself.

"Hurry! Get to the machine," called Clever to Peter, "Sarge will play with the doggie."

Play? Doggie? It's not exactly a cute little puppy, thought Peter, but he only took one last horrified look at Sarge bouncing between the ears before he hustled to the bulldozer and climbed up onto the crawler tracks to get to the engine cover. He couldn't help looking back to see if Sarge was still okay as he fumbled with the keys and the torch.

"What is taking so long?" asked Clever.

"Sorry, sorry," Peter muttered, his fingers shaking so much he took twice as long as normal to unlock the panel.

He finally managed to swing open the cover protecting the engine, pointing the torchlight at the metal, fuel lines, bolts and lugs, filter housings – and plenty of parts he couldn't identify – that made up the motor.

Weebit, Nimin, and Clever scrambled into position and inspected the workings before them. The other saboteur either hadn't tried to wreck the motor for a second time, or the dog had scared them off.

"Let's hop to it," said Clever, grinning up at Peter.

Nimin and Weebit didn't need telling twice. Snorting and giggling, they went to task on the metal lines and engine parts, while Clever disappeared from Peter's view towards the radiator at the front of the bulldozer. Very soon, pinging noises came from where he was attacking the back grill. Peter kept swivelling the torch to keep a worried eye on Sarge, wondering if he should open the cabin door so they could scramble in if the dog managed to brush him off. Being caught in the cabin by the workmen would be a nightmare, but being eaten by a Rottweiler was a more immediate problem. He had to admit, the dog seemed to be in more trouble than Sarge. It was becoming more and more frustrated, and he could see the white of sweat foaming on its flanks, its teeth snapping obsessively. Sarge was having a ball, cackling like he was on a roller coaster ride.

"C'mon, doggie. Ye ain't even tryin'!"

The dog seemed to be tiring but made another effort to free itself of its rider. Peter watched as, once more, it ran madly around the bulldozer, the chain clattering against the metal tread at the front of the crawler tracks. The dog raced past beneath where he stood, slowed briefly, and then butted its head into the crawler tracks near the rear, aiming to squash Sarge. There was a thud and the dog flopped, stunned. Sarge launched himself sideways and rolled away on the grass. He leapt to his feet and boldly patted the dazed animal on the snout before swaggering back towards the front of the bulldozer. The others had heard the noise and heads swivelled, Clever popping up from beneath the opening to see what was going on. Sarge quickly joined them and pouted because they had finished the job on the motor without his help.

"Let's get out of here," Peter said. He relocked the cover, they all scrambled down, and quickly headed back towards the woods. Peter saw Sarge sidle up to Clever's side as they walked and strained his ears to hear what they were saying.

"Hey, I want to keep the doggie," Sarge

said quietly.

Peter's mind boggled at the thought.

"What for?" asked Clever, shaking a disbelieving head.

"It'd be useful."

"You know you can't keep it. Where would you put it?"

"It can help me on patrol."

"And you accuse me of collecting wildlife," muttered Clever.

"I'd train it and care for it."

"We may not even have a home. And anyway, we don't keep pets."

"Yes we do! You have Peter," said Sarge. He glared at Clever and strode forward to walk with Nimin and Weebit. Clever carefully checked over his shoulder to see where Peter was and flushed beetroot when he found him to be within earshot. He shook his head and rolled his eyes in apology. Peter was just grateful he was still in one piece and walking away from the worksite and the dog.

#

Later that morning, the Dinglemen were keeping an eye on the worksite by themselves.

Peter had work that he needed to do at the clubrooms, and it had been over an hour since he had wound his way through the trees and disappeared in the direction of the club. Clever was settled comfortably on the pine needles to wait for the workmen to arrive and had a clear view of the site. The dog appeared to have recovered from its ordeal and was curled up asleep – nose under tail – near the front of the bulldozer. Sarge and Nimin were both looking restless. Sarge checked over his shoulder to see if Nimin was out of earshot and nudged Clever.

"Just look at that doggie's face, Clever. Isn't it cute."

"You can't see its face. Its nostrils are touching its—no, Sarge."

"Someone doesn't want it or they wouldn't have left it there. I bet we could train it to hunt."

"You know you can't have it."

"Playing with it might even toughen Nimin up."

"Not a chance."

"Look at it, it's lonely."

"Enough already."

Sarge was still muttering when they saw the

Hold-On roar up the road, complain loudly at leaping the ditch, and bounce to a stop. Even the sulking Sarge grinned at the look on the workmen's faces when they saw the state of the bulldozer. The human called Boggs howled in frustration, then stalked forward, shouting and swearing, towards the now cowering dog. Sarge stiffened at his side and Clever laid a restraining hand on his arm. Boggs swung his leg back to kick the dog with a heavy boot. He was stopped by the other one, Durdle, stepping in front of the dog.

"Get out of my way!" Boggs roared.

Durdle held his position. "No." His voice was flat.

Boggs turned and laid a vicious kick on the bulldozer, grimaced in rage and pain, glared at Durdle, and limped back to the Hold-On. Clever risked a sideways glance at Sarge. Sarge's eyes were bright and flicked between Boggs and the dog, which was now being patted on the head by Durdle. Sarge's gaze settled back on Boggs and his mouth curled into an evil smile.

"Keep your mind on our goal, Sarge."

"That's delightful coming from you, Mr. Research Scientist," Sarge hissed, but he stayed where he was.

"You'll get your chance to train the human."

Sarge nodded once in reply, his eyes still fixed on Boggs, and Clever turned his gaze back to see what the humans were doing. Boggs pulled something little out of the Hold-On, jabbed it with his fingers and talked at it. He finished talking, threw it down, and disappeared into the office for several minutes before backing out with a steaming cup and a collapsible chair. Another motorcar – a big, white, enclosed box with only a few small windows on the sides – pulled up, and the dog leapt to its feet. Durdle moved to untie the chain. The Dinglemen watched another human, dressed completely in navy clothes, walk over to the dog and pat its jubilant head. He murmured a few words to it as he led it to the open back of the motorcar. Sarge inhaled sharply when the dog leapt in and was lost from sight.

"Don't bring that useless thing back, either, or I'll kill it," Boggs called from his chair. The blue clothes human scowled at him, calmly got in the motorcar, and drove off. Sarge stared after the motorcar long after it turned from view. He briefly appeared crushed at his loss, sighed loudly, then straightened his shoulders and returned his attention to Boggs, who was lounging in his chair and sipping at his cup. Clever was just happy that Sarge had someone other than himself to take it out on. He could see a twitch in Sarge's jaw and that always meant trouble.

"Whew, I'm glad that doggie has gone. That doggie was mean," said Nimin, from behind them. Both Clever and Sarge whipped their heads around to glare at him.

"Whut? Whut'd I say?"

#

They met at their old meeting place just inside the woods along fairway fifteen, agreeing it was much safer than anywhere near the worksite where Boggs and Durdle would now be patrolling. A few humans were finishing a round of smacking balls about before it got dark, and they could be heard laughing or cursing as they passed, one letting out a bloodcurdling howl of frustration. There was the loud crack of a stick being snapped in two, then a barrage of more feverish swearing, which trailed off into bitter muttering as the human moved off.

"I really wish we knew something about these investors," said Peter.

"Yes, although I fear this is becoming dangerous," said Clever.

"I could take Boggs and Durdle down. It would be my pleasure," said Sarge.

Clever shook his head. "We wouldn't gain anything. They are getting another bulldozer and we can't prevent all of them from working."

"Mmmm, I'd like to know what makes them so scary," said Peter, still thinking about the investors.

"Yeah, but it would be my pleasure."

"We've failed," wailed Nimin, flopping against Weebit. Weebit took one surprised look at Nimin, and then his face crumpled and he sniffed miserably in harmony with Nimin.

"So we try Mr Smythe's office?" said Peter, ignoring Nimin and Weebit.

"Unfortunately, I can't think of a better alternative," said Clever.

"I could damage Boggs as a warning," offered Sarge.

Clever glared at him until Sarge smiled.

"Is that a no?" he asked, innocently.

Clever doubled his glare, then gave up against the grin and turned to Peter.

"I believe we are getting to the point in proceedings where we have to consider finding a new home," he said. Clever wasn't happy to say it, not after his dreams about the creation of this new Dingledell. "We must be realistic. It's not looking good, is it?"

Nimin and Weebit howled in unison.

"We won't give up yet," said Sarge. "We're not done here, and until we are done, we're not going anywhere."

Clever had the feeling Sarge was talking about dealing with Boggs, but at least Nimin and Weebit both brightened and stopped their snivelling.

CHAPTER ELEVEN

Over the next few hours, Boggs and Durdle came and went in the Hold-On, another motorcar arrived and a tool-carrying human walked over to the bulldozer, clicked his tongue, shook his head, and set to work fixing it. The black Mercedes Expensive, driven by the fat man, bounced onto the worksite causing Boggs and Durdle to leap to their feet. Clever knew the human was called Smythe or something, but could only think of him as the fat man. Just as he swung down from his motorcar, a red-faced and puffing Peter crept through the woods towards them. He whispered that he didn't want to miss what was said. The fat man stepped forward, paused and stared, stalked forward three steps, and then stopped and just gaped at the woods before him. Clever watched the blood drain from beneath his tan, his head swivelling back and forth along the trees. It was obvious to an observer that he hadn't yet heard about the new delays. He staggered backward and had to place a hand against his motorcar to stop from stumbling, his other hand waving disbelievingly at the trees. Boggs rushed towards him but stopped in his tracks at the vicious glare sent in his direction. Clever noticed that even Durdle looked unsettled as he moved to where the fat man was leaning against the motorcar. The fat man still stared at the worksite, not really believing his eyes. Then he straightened and croaked at the workmen. Clever wished he could hear what was being said. Unfortunately, from where the Dinglemen and Peter hid they could only make out a few phrases and words.

"—construction brought forward—won't understand—"

The human said something else while waving an arm, his face a picture of anxiety and rage, and then jabbed a finger at the middle of Boggs's face. Whatever was being threatened it must be bad, thought Clever. The fat man continued to talk animatedly as he and the workmen moved towards the front of the office. Sarge nudged Clever, one corner of his mouth twitching into a dry smile. Now they were closer, the Dinglemen and Peter could hear everything being said.

"You will have to guard the site tonight. All night," said the human. He spoke again over a protest from Boggs. "The dog was a waste of time. These people are obviously determined and resourceful, and we have to be ready for them. So guard the site. Or would you rather the investors dealt with you?"

Boggs didn't argue again.

"That's what I thought. And make sure you are both armed." He glowered at Boggs and Durdle to make sure they were still listening. "Fortunately for you, I've arranged for some more men and another bulldozer from tomorrow, so you can clear these trees in half the time. The investors can't know we are behind schedule. Do you understand me?"

The workmen nodded. The fat man glared at them again and stalked back to the Expensive. Peter whispered that he would meet the Dinglemen after he finished work and raced off, back the way he had come.

#

Peter set his alarm clock for midnight and tried to get a few hours rest. He needn't have bothered. He was too hyped to sleep and just tossed until the bed covers finally slid into a crumpled pile on the floor. He squinted at the clock. Twenty minutes to midnight. Near enough. He dressed in a black long-sleeved tee shirt and an old pair of black cargo pants, crammed a baseball cap onto his head, jammed a torch into his pocket and crept down the hall.

When he reached the clubrooms he waited near the storage shed, wishing the security lights weren't so bright. For a start, he could see there was fresh bird poop on the shoulders of Captain Breadalbone and he had only just cleaned him. He desperately hoped they would find what they needed inside Mr Smythe's office because he didn't want the Dinglemen to leave. They were his friends and they made him laugh, and he just couldn't picture the club without them anymore. Bending down to scratch an itchy foot, he pushed a finger down into the inside of his shoe. He was still trying to ease the itching when Clever stepped onto his foot and peered closely at what he was doing.

"Is there a switch in your shoe? What does it do?"

"No, I have an itch."

"Oh." Clever frowned. "Wouldn't it be wiser to remove the shoe to gain access to your foot?"

"Yep."

Clever looked at him expectantly.

"Uh, not right now, though. We have work to do," said Peter.

"Absolutely, yes, of course," said Clever. He hopped off the shoe and charged ahead towards the clubrooms. Sarge materialised beside Peter's foot.

"See what I have to put up with? He's unbearable."

Sarge walked after Clever, then looked back when Peter was slow to move.

"Well, hurry up then."

Peter was still smiling when he unlocked the back door, led the Dinglemen through and relocked it behind them. He left the Dinglemen near the door while he stepped quietly down the hallway to test the office. It was locked. Well, that was okay, he had been expecting that. Ushering the Dinglemen into the kitchen, he used his stool to climb up onto the table and placed the torch so it faced upward to shine on the ceiling tiles. He wished he could turn on the kitchen light but didn't think it was worth the risk. Passing cars might see the light and drive in to investigate. He lifted a tile, slid it sideways, and then held his hand down for Sarge to hop on, raising him up to the gap in the ceiling. Sarge had a long length of thin elastic cord looped over a shoulder and across his body, making him look a little bit like a wonky golf ball with legs.

"A bit closer," ordered Sarge.

Peter stood on tip-toes and stretched until Sarge could grip the edge of the neighbouring tile and boost himself through, his feet disappearing into the darkness above. They listened for him, but could hear nothing, as he travelled within the roof. Peter led the others down the hall towards Mr Smythe's office, the torch in one hand and tapping on the walls with the other to indicate to Sarge the direction to head. Peter continued to tap on the wall near the office, and then stopped to listen, tapped again. It felt as if an hour had passed, but by the seventh series of taps, Peter heard a small, breathless '*wheee*' from within the office. He smiled. It sounded as if the plan was working. Sarge had found his way through the ceiling. He would have then removed a tile near a beam in the roof, tied an end of the elastic to the beam, an end to his ankles, would probably have taken a deep breath, and jumped. Then he just needed to search in the bottom drawer. Hopefully, Mr Smythe hadn't thought to remove the spare key. Peter put his ear back against the door. Sarge was muttering, but at least it sounded as if the bungee had worked. After another few minutes of impatient waiting, listening to faint clattering from within, three keys were finally slid under the door.

"It's about time," grumbled Clever.

Peter tried the keys – the second one turning in the lock – opened the door and turned on the light. The office was on the other side of the clubrooms from the road so he figured it would be safe enough, and besides, they could search faster if they all looked. The Dinglemen fanned out, clambering onto the desk and levering their bodies into drawers. Peter smiled back at a grinning Sarge, who still looked flushed from his dive from the ceiling. He had done well. The elastic dangled just beside the edge of the desk, making it easy for Peter to replace the ceiling tile. He climbed up onto the desk, shoved the elastic up into the roof and slid the tile back into place, then helped the others with the search for useful information.

He took a proffered key from Weebit, who was standing waist deep amongst pens and paper clips in the desk top drawer, and tried the lock on the filing cabinet. It worked, and he slid the bottom drawer open to uncover a pile of golfing magazines and half a packet of chocolate biscuits. Not quite what they needed, Peter thought, peering over his shoulder to check that Nimin hadn't seen the biscuits. He tried the next drawer up, an ear cocked for noises other than the Dinglemen's ferreting. He ran a finger along the tabs on the manila folders in the next drawer – Fees, Accounting, Events, Advertising, Employee Payroll. He felt a brief urge to see what Caitlin and Daisy were paid, then pulled himself together and kept rifling through the drawer. Insurance policies, Equipment, Payroll, Catering.

BEEP BEEP BEEP!

Peter spun around, his eyes wide and heart pounding. Nimin was looking sheepish. He had leaned against a clock timer on the desk top. With the others frowning at him, Nimin pushed against the button and the beeping stopped. Peter turned back to the cabinet to resume his search, his heart rate only marginally slowing, a rustling on the desktop telling him the others were back to searching as well. Where had he gotten to? He walked his fingers backward. Catering. Payroll. Hang on, he thought, a second payroll? Well, he knew for certain he didn't get paid twice! He pulled out the two folders marked Payroll and flipped the first open on the desk. It was benign, filled with typical payroll information. He couldn't help himself, he had to look. Daisy was paid the same as him, but Caitlin made an extra three dollars an hour. Huh! He frowned and stuck out his lower lip. Closing the folder, he carefully put it back where he found it before opening the next one. The second Payroll folder yielded something even more interesting.

"Clever, look at this."

Clever was already on the desk and stepped onto the small pile of documents Peter laid down. He took a moment.

"Interesting, very interesting." He rubbed

his chin.

The other Dinglemen joined him and got shooed off by Clever. "Stand back, I need to read," he said. He stepped backward as he scanned each line, then hopped off the bottom of the first page and waved a hand for Peter to flip the paper over.

"Well?" said Sarge.

"These top pages are photocopies of recent newspaper clippings," answered Peter, "each about well-known criminals, mobsters, from the big city. I reckon I've seen some stuff on TV about these guys."

Clever continued to read. He was standing on a page of figures, moving from one line of numbers to another, striding down to the total where he shook his head, then returning to look again at the set of figures farther up the page.

"Peter, what does grass seed cost?" he asked, standing over a number halfway down the right hand edge of the page.

Peter peered at the number. "Whoa, not that much, surely."

"Hmm, what about this 'consultancy' fee, what would that be for?"

Peter shook his head. He had no idea. And

it was for tens of thousands of dollars, too. He spied the balance listed across from staff wages without Clever needing to point it out.

"We do not get paid that well! Nowhere near that well – even if we take Caitlin's three dollars an hour into account," he muttered.

Clever looked at him, waiting for him to explain. Peter shook his head ruefully and shooed Clever off the page, moving it to the side to see what else was in the pile of documents. Employee files. Normal looking employee files, with job titles, names, addresses, pay amounts – large pay amounts – bank details, tax file numbers, starting dates. The usual stuff, he guessed, aside from the level of pay. Peter did not know these people. They might be current staff on paper but he knew they didn't exist. And what was the point of that? Why make up extra staff? He lifted the last of the fake files, shuffling through the few remaining pages that were copies of invoices from McLeod Consultancy Services. The invoices looked real enough, but he had never heard of them. Peter looked closer at the page of figures. It looked like money going out from the club, payments for this and that.

Then something in his brain clicked into place, and he thought he knew what he was really looking at. Money laundering. Peter figured Mr Smythe was cleaning money received from illegal activities and filtering it through the club, taking a percentage and paying the rest to the mobsters. He bet the money paid into the fake employees' bank accounts was funnelled elsewhere immediately and the same went for the payments for the 'consultants'. Clever was way ahead of him.

"These bad men need the resort so they can exchange larger amounts of money, have a larger number of false employees. The club isn't big enough to hide the amounts they are receiving," said Clever.

"You're right, I'll bet if we—"

Peter broke off and listened. He had heard a scraping sound coming from near the side entrance of the club, the one nearest to the offices.

"Hide!"

He jammed the documents back into the folder, stuffed the folder back into the cabinet, threw the cabinet key in the top drawer, hit the light switch and raced behind one of the thick velvet curtains, making sure he was tight against the wall. He gave thanks for old fashioned furnishings and tried not to shake. His heart racing, he hoped the Dinglemen were better hidden than he was, then realised that that was a dopey thought, of course they were. It was him he should be worrying about.

#

Peter could hear footsteps rushing down the hallway. He sweated in his hiding spot as a key was jammed into the door, the light flipped on and someone bowled in, presumably Mr Smythe. Peter could hear the person move swiftly across the room to behind the large desk, a drawer being pulled open and the sound of a key being inserted into the filing cabinet. He closed his eyes and tried not to imagine being caught. He might have explained away being in the clubrooms but not behind a curtain in the office. He wished he could make a run for it but knew he had no chance to get past whoever was in the room. He wouldn't be able to unlock the window behind him fast enough, either. His legs were jelly and he was sure the curtain was vibrating with his shaking. Suddenly, Peter couldn't hear any more movement within the office and guessed the person had paused what they were doing and were now scanning the interior, looking for body shaped bulges in the curtains. He had thought his heart couldn't beat any faster, but he had been wrong. He was starting to feel nauseous. The person was going to look behind the curtains, for sure, and he would be in serious cacky. Then he heard a cabinet drawer being yanked open and the rapid rustling of papers.

The person made an audible sigh of relief and Peter guessed they held the Payroll folder. The same Payroll folder he would need to convince the police of what Mr Smythe and his 'investors' were involved in. The leather chair creaked as the person sat down. The telephone rang, and Peter screwed up his eyes and winced in a desperate effort not to make a sound as the receiver was snatched up.

"Yes, I'm listening." Mr Smythe's voice was low. Peter strained to hear, but couldn't even detect when the other person was talking, let alone hear anything they said.

"What have you done with her? I want to speak to her." There was another longer pause. "Yes, I—I understand." Another pause. "Yes, I'll be there."

Peter heard the handset being dropped back into the cradle, and the leather chair creaked again as Mr Smythe inhaled and exhaled a deep breath. Silence descended upon the room, making Peter want to scream, before eventually he heard Mr Smythe heading towards the door.

#

Peter was still too close to being discovered to celebrate his luck, even in his head. The light clicked off and the door slammed closed. He strained his ears to hear the key in the lock, and then the muffled sounds of footsteps hurrying down the hallway, before he dared to breathe out. He waited a further minute and then he peered from behind his curtain, the torch beam wavering as he scanned the room.

"Are you staying there all night?" asked Sarge, lounging against a desk leg with his arms crossed. Peter rolled his eyes and stepped out into the office. A timid Weebit was standing behind Sarge, ready to disappear again at a second's notice. At a faint noise near the filing cabinet, Peter turned the torch beam to find Clever scaling the drawers to where they had found the folder of evidence. He played the beam across the desk, across the floor, and back around the base of the curtains.

"Where's Nimin?"

"Could be anywhere, he'll come out when he's ready," said Sarge.

Peter walked across to the cabinet to help Clever, but he didn't think the folder would be there any longer. Mr Smythe had come back to collect his insurance policy against the mobsters. Why else keep something so incriminating? He wondered about the late night visit to the office, as he didn't think Mr Smythe was in his office much outside the hours of nine to five. He must have had a good reason to be out of bed at one in the morning.

Peter was right about the evidence. The second Payroll folder was gone. They had been so close to having proof, surely enough to shut down the resort, or at least enough to delay the work until it could be proven it was being built for illegal purposes.

"We had it," he muttered bitterly. He used the spare key to let them out, a wail coming from behind the leg of a guest chair as they left.

"Wait! Wait for me!"

CHAPTER TWELVE

As Peter crawled back into his bed and yanked the covers off the floor, he couldn't help wondering about who Mr Smythe had been talking to on the phone. Obviously, it was someone who knew where he might be found at that time of the morning. And it sounded as if they were planning to meet. Was it the workmen? And who had they been talking about?

Peter was late getting to work the next morning and was promptly told by one of the cleaners that he looked terrible. Was he coming down with something?

"I think I just need coffee," he grumbled.

"Well, a bit of a problem there, mate, unless you make your own."

Peter raised a questioning eyebrow.

"Caitlin didn't come in, some drama at

home. The boss called in sick, too."

Peter staggered off into the kitchen, which felt weird with only him in it and no inviting food smells. He sniffed experimentally. It smelt faintly of grease and lemon disinfectant, when it should have smelt like baking cakes and waffles and coffee.

He heard quick footsteps behind him and turned. A strange lady, with a shock of dyed red hair, barged past him and dropped grocery bags onto the table with a *whoosh* and a lot of rustling of plastic. Peter eyed the bags and wondered what Daisy would have to say about them when she arrived. If she was coming in. If she *was* coming in, he wouldn't want to be in the lady's shoes, he could just about imagine the length of the lecture.

"Good morning, dear!" the lady said, breezily. "Clara's the name!"

Peter blinked at her. Her hair was bright red. Her face was heavily powdered, with a lot of glittering blue eye shadow and a wide smear of orange lipstick. She looked as if she was maybe mid-fifties, and her red hair, the makeup and her clothes all made her look like a deranged fairy god mother. The impression was made even stronger when she giggled at him.

"It's bright hair I know, dear, I just love bright colours!" she said.

She wasn't joking, he thought. Her dress was a lime green, with little white flowers all over, she wore a sparkly lime cardigan, and her shoes had large silver buckles on them. He didn't think buckles like that had made it out of the middle ages.

He had to clear his throat. "Hi, um, I'm Peter."

Clara placed her hands on well-padded hips and rocked on the balls of her feet. "Well, of course you are dear. Be a doll and help me unpack these bags will you? There's a darling."

He attempted a sickly smile and did what she asked. He just hoped he could get out of the kitchen before he drowned in terms of endearment. Clara didn't seem to notice that he kept his head down and worked without replying to her chatter. Besides, he figured, he wouldn't be able to fit a word in even if he had been desperate to comment. Every gossipy sentence came at the speed of machine gun fire. She prattled away as she looked through the cupboards, commenting on the weather, fine, the traffic, horrific, the latest celebrity wedding, oh so tacky, the golf course, a bit run down, isn't it dear?

"—and such a worry about her sister isn't it?" He had been only half listening to her, but his head snapped up now.

"I'm sorry, what?"

"Caitlin's sister dear, I just wonder what this world is coming to, I really do."

"You mean Daisy? What's wrong with Daisy?"

"She's missing, haven't you heard?"

Peter froze. "Daisy's missing?"

"Well yes, dear, since this morning. She wasn't in her bed when her mother went to get her up, that's why Caitlin—"

"Excuse me!" He bolted from the kitchen, leaving Clara to gape after him.

#

He rode his bike into the car park of the nearest police station, out of breath and panting. Dumping the bike under a nearby tree, he rushed across the tarmac, pushed his way into the air-conditioned waiting room and strode to stand impatiently at the counter. He glanced around, feeling self-conscious and out of place in the large carpeted room. He had expected nightmarish posters on the walls, showing that bad things happen when people drink and drive, but that wasn't the case. Instead, the walls were mostly clean, with just one display cabinet filled with policemen's helmets. Some looked really old, and some looked really uncomfortable, and some looked both old and uncomfortable. He tried to peer into the enclosed office to see if anyone was in there, and tapped the bell sitting in front of him on the counter. There was only one other person seated in the room, a large older woman dressed in shabby black who scowled at him when he glanced at her. He faced the desk again, and for the second time, thumped the bell for service.

"All right, keep your hair on, buddy." A tall and solid uniformed man strolled into the office from the hallway behind, flicking through a pile of mail that he held in his large hands. He carefully placed the stack of envelopes on a desk before humming his way over to the counter. Only then did he look down at Peter.

"Hello, you're a bit young to be confessing, ain't you?" The policeman grinned at his own joke, crow's feet crinkling the corners of his eyes. Peter wondered how often the policeman had said that line before.

"How can I help you, young man?"

Now that he was here, and on the spot, Peter's mind emptied. There was a smear of tomato sauce clinging to the policeman's moustache and that wasn't helping him gather his thoughts, either. He stammered out that he needed to speak to someone about the missing girl, Daisy Keller. Rushing his words, he explained that he thought he knew who had kidnapped her.

"You do, eh?" The policeman raised an eyebrow.

Inwardly, Peter groaned. Convincing people of anything was near impossible when they gave you the look the policeman was currently giving him.

"Okay then, what's your name?"

"Peter. Peter Birdwell."

"Kidnapping is a serious business—"

"Please, I really do have information. I'm not here for some prank." Peter looked as earnest as he could. The policeman sighed, but told Peter to stay put and disappeared back out the door he had entered with the mail. Peter waited for another age, and just when he decided he had been forgotten, a door in the corner of the room opened and a different, much younger policeman's head poked through.

"Peter, is it? You'd better follow me."

The young policeman held the door open for him and ushered him down a hall into a sterile meeting room that contained only a plain table and chairs. An empty styrofoam cup perched on the edge of the table, and fine dust particles swirled in the shafts of sunlight streaming through old venetian blinds. The young policeman waved him to a chair and slid himself into the one closest to the door. His expression was that he had drawn the short straw and he knew it.

"I'm Constable Denton. What information do you have to share with us, Peter?"

Peter closely watched the constable's face as he told what he knew about Mr Smythe and the workmen, and his suspicions about the mobsters being the investors, explaining that he had seen the second payroll folder by accident. He outlined what it contained.

"And what were you doing looking in a payroll folder? I'm assuming you don't have anything to do with the office administration, do you? You said you work on the grounds."

"Um, yeah," Peter felt himself turn pink. "I wanted to know if my friends and I were earning the same wages. We had a competition running. You know, about who earned the most for the season?"

"Uh-huh." The policeman didn't look convinced or amused. "What makes you think the club manager would be involved with Daisy's disappearance?"

"I was there last night, about one in the morning."

"That's very late for you to be at work, isn't it? Did your parents know where you were?"

"Well, um, I'd left my wallet in the kitchen and I was worried about it—" Peter paused to see how well Constable Denton swallowed his fib, hoping he wouldn't press the question.

"Uh-huh, sure. Go on."

"Um, well, I overheard a voice in the office, but the hallway lights were off, which seemed strange. So I crept down the hall to see who it was, but I stayed quiet because it might have been burglars or anyone."

"That was a bit foolhardy, don't you think?"

"I guess. Anyway, it was Mr Smythe talking on the phone, and he asked the other person what they had done with 'her' and it had to be Daisy he was talking about, and she could be hurt and—"

"Did you hear him say her name?"

"No, but—"

"Did you hear him say anything about kidnapping? Or worse?"

"No."

"Did he say anything about where they were keeping this person they were talking about?"

"No."

"Where they were taking them?"

"No, but Mr Smythe—"

"You seem very interested in the worksite," Constable Denton cut him off.

"Um, yeah. I like bulldozers."

The policeman's mouth turned down and he leaned forward. "You like bulldozers? You wouldn't happen to know anything about the worksite bulldozer being sabotaged, do you? The destruction of property is a very serious incident, you know."

"No, sir, I don't know anything about that," squeaked Peter.

Constable Denton watched him patiently for several seconds, and then finally asked, "Do you have anything further to add?"

"No, but I do know Mr Smythe—"

The constable held up his hand and Peter trailed off.

"We'll look into it. You get back to work at the club and leave the detective work to the experts, okay? That's our job." He stood and opened the door. "We'll take care of it, Peter. Hey, maybe in several years' time you might consider joining the force, huh?" he said.

Peter was ushered out of the station, the constable even opening the glass doors for him, and reminding him as he picked up his bike. "Leave finding Daisy to us, Peter. Don't do anything that might get you into trouble."

Peter wheeled his bike out to the road, feeling fed up with the whole morning. And how well did that go? But he wouldn't give up on Daisy, he decided, as he threw a leg over his bike. He knew Mr Smythe's friends had Daisy locked away somewhere, and with help from the Dinglemen he was going to do something about it. And somehow, he would show that Mr Smythe and his investors were laundering money – he just had to work out how to get hold of the proof. Daisy first, though. He had left his bike in a low gear and he wobbled off back to the club, muttering under his breath as he pushed hard against the pedals.

He didn't go straight back to work. First, he detoured past the worksite, which was now teeming with yelling men and roaring equipment. The woods didn't stand a chance against the onslaught and there was already a swathe of felled trees, leaving ruptured earth where they had once stood. He shook his head dismally at the scene before him. At the rate the trees were falling, he guessed the Dinglemen's home would be gone by tomorrow afternoon. As he watched, Peter came to a realisation. Of course! Stupid, stupid! He would bet that Daisy had been the other saboteur, doing her bit for the environment, and she had managed to get herself caught by Boggs and Durdle. He sighed and made to push off. As he did, he spotted Boggs walking across the clearing towards the office. He didn't see Durdle anywhere.

#

Clever carefully folded a pair of leggings onto the top of his backpack and fastened the ties, glancing over as he did so to watch Nimin cram pots and clothes into his backpack in a mix of dented metal and material. Dirty leggings were stuffed into a small pot sitting by his side. Clever grimaced, thinking that he had to eat food cooked in that pot. Nimin looked so miserable at his task, though, that Clever didn't have the heart to comment. He knew how Nimin felt because he was miserable, too. They had seen the group of humans and the machines arrive at the worksite earlier and knew it was only a short matter of time before Dingledell was destroyed.

Leaving his backpack sitting where it was, he trudged up the completed stairs to his favourite spot on the lookout branch. Weebit was already there, staring through the branches in the direction of the distant sounds. Clever stood in the entrance to the lookout, gazing past Weebit and finding that he, too, was transfixed by the distant growling and cracking of tortured wood. He felt like crying for those trees, for Dingledell, for Weebit and Nimin and Sarge, and for himself.

He pulled his attention back to their tree, running his hand along the rough bark of the balcony's outer rim, turning to peer up into the leaves that would have given shade and protection from the weather. Nimin's red umbrella was leaning near the doorway, waiting to be opened up to give extra shade. Clever gulped. He didn't want to find a new home. He didn't want to be packed and ready to leave. He wanted to be able to sit out here peacefully, maybe shaded by the umbrella, watching butterflies fluttering on nearby leaves and watching sparrows flit past.

"It's time we met up with Peter. Let's go." Sarge spoke briskly from behind him, then turned and clattered back down the staircase. Clever and Weebit exchanged glances but trailed down the stairs in his wake. As much as they hated to leave, they didn't want to get on the wrong side of a prickly Sarge at that moment. He was taking the situation as poorly as the rest of them and was in a foul mood.

They reached the edge of the woods in time to see Peter in the distance, rapidly heading in their direction. As he grew closer, Clever could see he was puffing and sweaty.

They waited until he ducked through the outer row of trees and sat in his usual spot, leaning against a tree trunk that gave him a partial view across the nearest fairway. Clever still felt odd trying to think of it as a fairway rather than a field. It occurred to him that he wouldn't have to worry about golfing names soon and he felt a great sense of loss.

"We have to leave," he blurted to Peter. It came out more as a wail than a statement.

"Yeah, I know, I rode past the worksite," said Peter. There was a pause as they all listened to the rumbling noises in the distance. Peter caught his breath before he went on, "Guys, I think they've kidnapped a girl I know, Daisy. She works in the kitchen at the club."

"Daisy?" asked Clever. "The bossy one?"

Peter looked at him, surprised, "You know her?"

Clever thought back to his research, following Daisy, and the couple of humans she berated during their bonding ceremony.

"I believe I do."

"I should have worked it out earlier and then maybe I could have stopped her." Peter shook his head. "She's keen on protecting the environment. I think she's the other saboteur. She was probably trying to save the woods." He frowned. "Although, you know, really, I thought placards and chaining herself to a tree would be more her style." Shaking his head again, he rushed his next words. "And now she's been caught and I don't know what they've done with her, but I didn't see Durdle at the site and I'll bet he's guarding her somewhere. Remember when Mr Symthe was talking about 'her' last night. It had to be about Daisy. The workmen have put her somewhere and she could be in danger."

He told them about his morning, starting with the human called Clara, then about his trip to the police station. Clever wanted to know more about the function of 'police' but he got the general idea when Peter said they were a bit like Sarge. Sarge just smirked at him. Peter explained how the police hadn't seemed that interested in hearing about Mr Smythe or the investors. By the time they got onto the right track it might be too late.

"I'm going to try to find Daisy myself. And, well, I know you have your own problems, but will you help me?"

Sarge grinned nastily. "Boggs will be there,

won't he?" He nodded and pursed his lips. "I have a few lessons to share with Boggs. Count us in."

Clever rolled his eyes but nodded with the others. Of course they would help, and at least Sarge's mood would improve while he had heads to bang together. They agreed the best plan of attack was to follow the workmen, and that they should be there when the workmen finished for the day, to follow Boggs and hope he led them to where Daisy was being held.

#

Sarge was humming and striding out ahead of the others, vaulting over roots in his path and looking the happiest he had been in days. Behind him, Clever looked down at his tunic and sighed. Sarge had taken his best spotlessly-clean white tunic and dyed it a hideous dark green. His best tunic! He eyed the others as they swept over the pine needles, and knew he was as well camouflaged as they were, although he didn't see the point. Sarge said it was all about mental preparation. Clever thought that maybe Sarge was enjoying himself just a bit too much. By the time Sarge had let them leave Dingledell, each was dressed in dark green from head to foot and they all had their faces blackened. They were going into battle Sarge had reminded them, although Clever had only finally, reluctantly, sacrificed the tunic to avoid upsetting Sarge's new easygoing mood. Each had a piece of dark green cloth tied around their heads and knotted at the side, apart from Weebit whose head covering completely hid his red hair. They tested their camouflage on Peter, Sarge smiling when it took him much longer than usual to spot them, and then gaping at them when he did see them.

In the distance, the sound of the machines died. Peter looked at his watch and said it was twenty to five.

"Drat!" he said, "I didn't think they'd stop work until after five. I wanted to be in position." He took off through the trees, calling over his shoulder. "Come on. We'll have to run."

Clever and the others easily overtook him and raced ahead before he had run past the next few trees. They stopped as one, gawping in horror at the carnage. Clever could hardly believe the damage that had been done already. Puffing hard, Peter caught up with them and urged them forward over freshly piled earth, amongst raw exposed roots, around fallen trunks, over cracked branches and torn leaves.

They only slowed when they came up behind the retreating backs of the last of the workmen to leave for the day. The very last man dawdled over picking up his gear, and then sauntered after the others at a pace only marginally faster than stationary. There was no way they could wait for him to catch up to the others before they moved. Clever glanced at Peter in apprehension. The Dinglemen were able to follow the workmen without a problem but Peter was harder to keep hidden. Clever winced as Peter briefly became exposed, creeping parallel to the last workman while inching forward between the cover of fallen tree trunks. Peter's luck held and he slipped behind the first of the bulldozers. He was moving forward as quickly and quietly as he could, but somehow Peter had to get onto the Hold-On before Boggs left, and Clever didn't know how he would be able to do that. Who would want to be the lumbering size of a human?

Clever caught a glimpse of the other workmen, already collecting bags, boxes and whatever else from beside the office, talking loudly about some team of players. Peter paused, crouched behind a motorcar parked near the machines, a similar size to the Hold-On but with a flat rear half. With the others, Clever scooted up behind him and they stood near his feet to watch the workmen. He looked up at Peter's face.

"Flatbed ute," Peter whispered.

Clever nodded knowledgeably. Then his heart jumped when he saw the surly Boggs peel away without a word to anyone and stalk towards the line of motorcars waiting to take the humans home.

"Sarge!" Peter hissed. "I don't know how but stop Boggs! Don't let him drive off."

Sarge snapped off a salute and was gone, travelling fast along the back of the office and disappearing around the corner towards where Boggs was headed.

"Ow! M'foot!" Boggs bellowed and fell into loud cursing.

The heads of the workmen turned to look at Boggs and Peter took the opportunity to scuttle across to hide behind the office, the others joining him to peer around the corner. Boggs was near the front of the parked motorcars and was sitting on the ground, gripping his foot in both hands. The other workmen walked over to see what was up with Boggs and stood in front of him with their backs to the motorcars, blocking his view with their legs. Clever heard Peter suck in a breath, before he sprinted the short distance to squat down behind the back of a blue motorcar. Peter peeked back around the tyre to check on the workmen. He hadn't been noticed.

"Let's go," said Clever.

Nimin and Weebit took off ahead of him, to speed past where Peter was keeping low and waddling on haunches along the row of motorcars. Clever overtook Peter and met with Sarge and the others behind a rear wheel of the Hold-On to wait for him. Peter hunched down near them, tested the rear door, smiled when he found it unlocked and swung it open. The Dinglemen skittered up into the back and got out of the way in time for Peter to land heavily behind them. He hurriedly slammed the door, pulled a waterproof coat over himself and the Dinglemen, hunkered down and hid from view as much as he could.

"All here?" asked Peter quietly.

"Yes, we're here," Clever answered for the others.

"Thanks Sarge. Good job."

"Anytime, just say the word." Sarge sounded pleased.

There was a thump as Boggs threw something in the back next to Peter. Nimin squeaked and Clever felt Sarge elbow him to keep him quiet. Then the rear door slammed, the Hold-On rocked as Boggs climbed up into the driver's seat, the front door thonked shut and the engine roared to life. The motorcar rolled forward, lurched over the ditch and turned left, away from the city. After a few minutes, Clever felt the Hold-On turn to the right, run straight for several more minutes, left, right again, and after a while he gave up trying to remember the turns. The sound of the road beneath the spinning wheels was a smooth, hypnotic drone, and Clever was perfectly comfortable, leaning against Peter's arm and breathing in the warm smell of oiled leather and brushed cotton from the coat. He was thankful it didn't smell of Boggs. Clever idly wondered how much longer they'd be travelling.

CHAPTER THIRTEEN

Peter thought they might be on a highway, judging by the zoom of passing cars, and he had heard a few big trucks whoosh past, heading in the opposite direction. He felt the Jackaroo slow, then pull off the road and roll to a stop. Boggs yanked on the handbrake and got out. Peter risked a quick peek out the dusty side window and saw they were at a service station with an attached fast food outlet. He couldn't see the service station name, and was desperately looking for some clue to tell him where they were, but had to duck down when a car pulled in behind the Jackaroo. He just couldn't risk being seen. He lay quietly, not daring to raise his head again, and it was only a few minutes before Boggs climbed back in, rustling a plastic bag of supplies. The smell of warm food wafted over to the back, and Peter put a hand around where he thought Nimin was, just in case.

The Jackaroo moved off again, the radio flipped on and Boggs started to sing along to *Dancing Queen* in a pleasant tenor voice. Under his jacket, Peter tried not to snort too loudly. Who would have thought? Not only could Boggs sing, he had an unlikely taste in music. Peter bit his lip when the next song came on and Boggs's volume went up a notch to *It's Raining Men*.

Peter felt them judder over a bridge and continue, motoring up a curving hill, then the feeling of tipping, his head below his feet as they drove down the other side. It was several minutes later that Peter felt the Jackaroo turn onto an unsealed road, and for the first time he seriously questioned what he was doing hiding in the back of Boggs's vehicle. They had been driving for at least an hour, and this was feeling more and more like a really bad idea. How remote was this place? It had to be where they were keeping Daisy. The Jackaroo slowed and turned a hard right, before trundling along what felt like a very overgrown, rough and potholed track. Under the jacket, Peter sensed trees were casting shadows over the vehicle, and then they broke out into open and the Jackaroo juddered to a halt. He could hear Boggs snatch up the plastic bag at the same time as the door opened, felt Boggs climb out, heard the door slam shut. Peter waited until he thought Boggs would be far enough away from the Jackaroo before he peeled back the jacket and slowly raised his head to carefully peer around.

They were parked in the dusty open yard of an old farmhouse, the surrounding grounds covered in long, brown grass, scrubby bush and rocks. Boggs wasn't to be seen, and Peter guessed he must have already entered the small two-storeyed farmhouse. He was surprised Boggs had been able to walk across the wonky verandah without stepping through, as the boards were warped and cracked and looked rotten. They had probably never seen a coat of paint or varnish. The house itself was layered with yellowed white paint, peeling in patches to reveal a flaky pale green undercoat, and in some places the bare boards underneath. The place was a dump. From inside the back of the Jackaroo, he could see a little orchard just behind the house and even the trees were aged and gnarled with neglect. He didn't know this place, or how he was going to get away from here. But, first things first, he thought. Find Daisy.

"Well? Where are we," hissed Sarge.

"A farmhouse," Peter whispered back. "Have a look."

The four Dinglemen scaled over the pile of bags and junk lying in the back to stand lined up on the side of the Jackaroo, viewing the property before them through the side window. Over their heads, Peter could see a large red barn and a number of smaller sheds sprinkled behind the house. Daisy could be in any one of them or in the house itself.

Peter did a quick check of the farmhouse for signs of Boggs or Durdle before jumping down from the back of the Jackaroo and slinking across to stand flat against the peeling side of the building. Up close, it smelt faintly of mould. Layered over the mould was the smell of barbeque, the aroma wafting from an open window just above Peter's head. Boggs must be cooking his dinner. The Dinglemen had followed and were skulking around Peter's feet, and judging by the wrinkled noses and lip smacking, they had smelt the cooking meat, too.

"Are we going in?" asked Nimin, his eyes the size of dinner plates. Peter knew it was a dinner plate that Nimin had in mind.

"Yes," agreed Sarge, "we should pay Boggs a visit."

"I concur," said Clever, "we haven't eaten since lunch. Peter, you stay here and we'll check on Boggs."

"Guys, we don't know if he's alone."

"So?" said Sarge.

"Well, we can't afford to get caught. What if you get caught?"

The Dinglemen just stared at him, their expressions ranging from gaping surprise to an outright smirk. Peter tried to think fast.

"Fine, yes, okay. You don't have a problem with avoiding capture, but I do. Besides, we don't know that Daisy is in the house, and we need to check the other buildings first. Yes, that's what we should do." He blundered away from the house towards the nearest shed and hoped the Dinglemen would follow.

The first outbuilding was a squat, once-white painted brick shed that he didn't think was a likely place for a prison. It was too derelict, too overgrown and too bare. The grizzling Dinglemen caught up with him as he stood on his toes to peer through the remains of the window pane. He was right. Nothing was inside but a pile of ancient rubbish, a rusted bath tub, a dirt floor and a spider convention.

"C'mon guys, let's try the barn."

There was more grumbling from behind him as Peter walked carefully towards the red barn. From where he stood, he could see the Jackaroo parked in the yard, and he had a line of sight to the nearest corner of the farmhouse verandah. Once again, he circled around to the back of the barn and stretched to see in through a small window. The barn was in much better repair than the brick shed but the window was too dirty for him to see through. Even when he used the bottom of his tee shirt to wipe a circle he just smeared the grime around and could only see shadows inside.

"Well?" asked Clever.

"I can't see. I'll have to try a side window."

There was a sudden movement in the long grass a few metres away from them, and when Peter shifted from the window a rabbit appeared, watching him warily. Nimin grinned, whooped and took off towards the rabbit. It darted away through the grass with Nimin right behind.

"Nimin!" Sarge growled.

Clever rolled his eyes. "Peter, we'll be back in a minute."

The Dinglemen sped off after Nimin.

Shaking his head, Peter crept towards the corner of the building and around the side to find a better window. He slid along the warm boards of the side of the barn, painfully aware that he must stand out against the red paint in his white tee shirt and dark blue shorts. The side window was placed lower and was much larger than the one at the back. He had to rub this window as well, smearing more grime around, but finally managing to clear a patch to peer through. He shielded the sides of his eyes with his hands and concentrated on the interior. He could make out the shape of an old tractor parked on the opposite side of the barn and hanging shapes that looked like tools of some kind. He squinted. There was, maybe, what looked like a pile of hay bales stacked in the far corner and a wheelbarrow in front of the stack. He couldn't see enough of this side of the barn so he shuffled sideways, squashing his face against the old glass to get a better look. Peter froze when he felt a hand land on his shoulder.

"What are you doing here?" said Durdle, quietly. "Peter, why couldn't you keep out of this?"

Boggs's voice called for Durdle from the front of the barn, "What are you doing? Stop mucking around."

Boggs put his head around the corner to see what Durdle was up to, and now he swaggered towards them. Peter felt ill, and risking a glance at Durdle, saw only a blank expression.

"Well, well, well. What have we here?"

Peter managed a squeak, wondering where Sarge was when he needed him. Boggs cocked his head and looked steadily at Durdle. Then he ordered Durdle to be useful and feed the girl, while he, Boggs, would deal with the boy. Somewhere under the layers of terror a small part of Peter punched the air in triumph. Yes, he knew it! He knew it was them who kidnapped her! The rational part of Peter became sarcastic. Oh, well done, Sherlock, he told himself. Brilliant deduction. And getting caught here was a genius move.

Boggs growled at him. "You are in big trouble, boy."

Roughly gripping his shoulder, Boggs frog-marched Peter to the front of the barn where the main door had been partially slid aside, leaving a man-width opening into the dark interior. Peter could hear low voices coming from inside the barn. Then, clearly, a girl's voice raised in disgust.

"Fast food, again! What're you trying to do? Slowly poison me to death? Do you know how full of fat and sugar and salt this stuff is? Man, this is gonna—"

It wasn't the right voice but she certainly sounded like Daisy. Boggs shoved Peter through the door and the girl broke off her tirade and blinked at him. Peter recognised her as Camilla, Mr Smythe's daughter.

Boggs signalled Durdle to pull over a solid wooden chair and a length of rope from behind the ancient tractor. He pushed Peter down hard on the chair, digging blackened nails under his collar bone to force him to sit. Peter tried to struggle against being tied up and felt a solid palm slap hard across the back of his head.

"Ow."

"Then stop wriggling." Boggs tied Peter's wrists behind him, looped the rope through the chair back, roped his feet to the front legs, and gave the rope a final yank to tighten the knots.

"Ow!"

"Shaddup," Boggs growled, "and as for you, miss," he strode over to the door before finishing his sentence, "you should eat the food and be grateful for it. It might just be your last meal." He marched out. Durdle widened his eyes at Peter in apology before gently sliding the door closed, casting the interior of the barn into gloom.

"That guy has weird eyes," said Camilla.

#

Clever and the others paused at the edge of the shadow cast by the barn. Where was Peter? They had only been gone for a few minutes and now here they were and Peter had disappeared. Sarge nudged Clever and nodded in the direction of the farmhouse, from where there was the sound of footfalls clomping across the porch.

"He's not being very careful, is he?" said Clever. "Boggs will hear him, surely."

"Come on," said Sarge. He led them across the grass, and they stopped at the corner of the farmhouse while he quickly scaled a drainpipe to peer onto the porch. Peter had gone and the door was shut. Sarge shook his head.

"He's gone inside without us!" said Nimin. "I can't believe he would do that. He must want the food for himself and he's not going to share." His voice rose as he spoke. "And I'm hungry, too!"

"Shhhh. Keep it down." Sarge glared at him.

"Let's find another way in," said Clever.

Weebit had already walked under the porch while Nimin spoke and now he disappeared into the gloom as he headed towards the other side of the house. By the time the others caught up with him, he was scrambling through a rat sized hole in the bottom plank to gain access under the house. Clever sighed and looked down at his tunic again. At least the dirt wouldn't show up so much against the dark green, he supposed, but he really wished they could pretend to be civilised for once and use a door. He sighed again and followed the others. Once he was under the house, Clever carefully inched forward and immediately walked into a spider's web, whirling his arms to break the strands and frantically wiping at his face. He only stopped wiping when he noticed Sarge was watching him and smiling. Clever stared back with his best deadpan expression, grimaced, and picked his way through the rusted cans and rubbish, crusted dirt, spider webs, coils of wire and dirty glass jars to stand just behind where the others had gathered.

"What? Why have you stopped?"

Sarge pointed at a narrow patch of daylight against the dirt, which indicated a hole in the floorboards above them, then raised his finger and pointed up. Clever looked up. The board was half missing, giving them easy access into the house. Clever couldn't tell if the damage was made recently. He thought it was possible Boggs had walked too heavily on the old floors. Sarge walked away and rummaged amongst the junk piled beneath the house. He came back over with a long, thin piece of metal and propped it carefully against the lip of the hole above them, tested it once to make sure it wouldn't move, then used it as a ramp. He stuck his head up through the hole, checked the coast was clear, and gestured for the others to follow.

Clever looked around the room they had entered. It was at the back of the house and had probably been a sleeping room, although it was empty of furniture and didn't feel as though it had been slept in for a long time. The walls were covered with rose-printed paper, but it was stained with mould and in places it bubbled away from the wall behind. The rest of the floor looked as rotten as the board that had broken.

Inside the house, the smell of cooking food was even stronger, and Clever put his hand on his stomach to quieten a rumble. Sarge moved the short distance to the door with Nimin right on his heels, paused to check for danger, and melted out of the room. Clever and Weebit caught up with them when they stopped at the entrance to the front part of the house, a wide hallway behind them and a partially open doorway ahead. Sarge turned to glare at Nimin until he crookedly smiled an apology and stopped shoving into his back. Clever leaned around Sarge to peer into the room. Boggs was seated on a folding chair, pulled up to a small wooden table, knife and fork in his hands, and his attention on a plate in front of him. He was busy shovelling his dinner into his mouth. Peter wasn't in the room, but the food smelt good.

"You want more spuds?" someone called from the next room. Sarge and Clever exchanged glances as they watched Durdle come into view carrying a pan and wearing a purple cover over his clothes that was tied in a bow at the back. Nimin sniffed loudly in Clever's ear, his beady eyes glued to Durdle as he put more food onto Boggs's plate.

"Take that stupid apron off," growled Boggs, "you look ridiculous."

"So? It protects my clothes," said Durdle. Clever was interested. He could do with one of those apron garments. He made a mental note to design one for himself. Durdle retreated into the next room with the pan and Boggs went back to shovelling.

"Here's the plan," whispered Sarge. He prodded Nimin in the chest with two fingers, indicated the plate, prodded Weebit and Clever and pointed at the floor to direct them to stay put, then pointed at his own chest and through to what was probably the kitchen, leading to the front of the house. They all nodded they understood and watched Sarge skulk around the door, along the wall and out of view. They waited. Finally, there was a loud crash from somewhere near the front door. Boggs leapt to his feet and thundered in the direction of the noise. Nimin darted onto the table, where he selected his choice off Boggs's plate. He carted a large piece of steak and a napkin, back to where Clever and Weebit were standing. Nimin dropped the steak on the napkin, checked around the corner, and was back on the table in a second. This time, a red sauce bottle raced across the floorboards towards the doorway.

"Boggit," muttered Clever, "I bet that's tomato."

Durdle ambled into their view, carefully carried his own laden plate to the other end of the little table and sat down to eat. Sarge slipped past and joined the others around the steak, waving at Nimin to pour more sauce on the top until it dribbled over the sides.

A few minutes later, Boggs returned. Clever leaned against the wall next to Sarge, the door slightly ajar so they could help themselves to their steak and still keep an eye on Boggs and Durdle.

"Nothing. I checked the barn, too, and it's all as it should be." Boggs sat back down, picked up his knife and fork, and froze.

"Durdle?"

Durdle had his mouth full, and he looked over innocently. "Mmmm?"

"Did you take my steak?"

"Pardon?" Durdle stopped chewing.

"I said, did you eat my steak?" Boggs's voice was sharp.

"Of course not." Durdle gestured at his plate with his knife. "I have my own."

"If you wanted more, you should have cooked more," said Boggs, his face turning a shade of purple to match Durdle's apron. He lunged out of his folding chair and leaned forward over the table, his face shoved close into Durdle's. Durdle didn't react.

"I did not take your steak," he said, mildly. "But, if it is that important to you, you can have mine."

"I don't want your leftovers." Boggs grunted, shoved the table aside, leaned back and telegraphed a huge swinging punch, giving Durdle plenty of time to rock his chair backward and out of the way. Sarge grinned at Clever.

"How lucky are we? Dinner and a show!"

Durdle let his chair rock forward again, without leaping aside or standing, and made no attempt to move when Boggs gripped his shirt with bunched fists and snarled in his face. Cold and unblinking, Durdle's eyes drilled back into his, and something in their depths caused Boggs to pause, face still only centimetres away from Durdle's. Neither moved for several seconds. Boggs finally rumbled in his throat, released his grip, and backed away.

"I'm going for a walk," he growled, and stormed out of the room. He slammed the front door as he left and caused a mild shower of dust and paint flakes in the hallway where the Dinglemen were dining. Expressionless, Durdle pulled the table back across, straightened the salt and pepper containers, swept up the few stray peas and deposited them on Boggs's plate. He aligned his own dinner, arranged a napkin across his lap, and forked up mashed potato and peas.

"Show over," muttered Sarge, wiping his mouth on an edge of the napkin. "Let's go find Peter."

#

"Do I know you?" asked Camilla.

"No, I don't think so," said Peter, his thoughts flitting to his model plane still sitting on his desk with a busted wing.

"You seem familiar. Anyway, what are you doing here?" said Camilla. She was sitting on the floor with her knees tucked up, squeezing her body into a corner made by the wall and a bed frame. Very pale, she had dirt-streaked tear stains on her cheeks and a bit of hay stuck in her mussed hair. Peter figured it would be rude to tell her that she looked like a scarecrow.

"Um, let's just say I was in the wrong place at the wrong time," he said, and grimaced, feeling embarrassed and sure he had turned pink. He looked into Camilla's gloomy corner, just below the window he had tried to peer through earlier. She had a chain cuffed around her ankle, which looped through a bolt in the wall, giving her just enough movement to shift a few metres in each direction.

They hadn't bothered to tie her hands, and someone had provided a rickety spring bed, a grey blanket and a blue fluffy pillow. Peter guessed the pillow was a Durdle touch.

"Are you okay?" he asked.

She looked at him scornfully instead of replying. Then she looked down at her shackled feet and burst into tears.

"We'll be all right, Camilla." He didn't quite know how to deal with the tears, realising he preferred the scorn, so they sat in silence for several minutes. There was a sound at the door, it slid aside and Boggs stuck his head in, checked they were both still where they should be, and slammed the door shut again.

"What was that about?" said Peter. "Do they check on you every half hour?"

Camilla shook her head. "Not before now."

"Why you? Why did they kidnap you?"

"I don't know! Nobody else was home yet. And that one with the googly eyes, he's been in my bedroom!"

"You weren't sabotaging the worksite at the golf course?"

"Of course not. Why would I do that?" The scorn was back.

They both heard furtive footfalls near the door and exchanged glances. The roller door was inched across and Mr Smythe oozed into the barn.

"Daddy!"

"Hello, pumpkin. Keep your voice down."

It was then that Mr Smythe noticed Peter. He blinked in surprise but quickly recovered.

"Well, hello there, Peter. Caught snooping, were you? That's too bad."

Mr Smythe hurried over to Camilla, pursed his lips at the shackles, hissed "I'll be back," and disappeared out of the barn. He returned with a small tool box, released his daughter, and hustled her out of the barn.

"What about me?" asked Peter.

"Oh, don't worry, Peter, I'll be back in a minute." Mr Smythe winked at him.

#

He kept his word. Moments later he was back, shoving a pale, bruised and sobbing Daisy ahead of him.

"Daisy!"

"Quiet," hissed Mr Smythe, "or I will hurt her, do you understand me?" Daisy sagged in his grip, but he easily carted her across and shackled her in Camilla's place.

"What? Why?" asked Peter.

"I found this young lady on my worksite." He seemed to be thinking out loud as he stood up. "She shouldn't have been there." He moved past Peter on his way to the door. "And, you know, I really haven't known what to do with her. This is perfect, don't you think?" He smiled at Peter. "Besides, the police will be looking for Daisy. It wouldn't be polite to disappoint them."

"I know what you've been up to at the club."

"Really, Peter? I'd be surprised if that were true. Not that it matters now, though, does it? Because you are staying here, aren't you? Bye bye, now." He smiled again and left.

"Daisy, are you okay?"

Daisy glared at him and Peter felt a sense déjà vu.

"So he caught you at the worksite? What then?"

"I've been stuck in some tool shed, and then he stuffed me into the boot of his car and brought me here. I think he followed the workman."

Who knew that Boggs was the pied piper, thought Peter. He sighed and fell silent.

It was a few minutes later, when Peter's

eyes rested on the bag of food still sitting untouched near Daisy that a synapse finally sparked.

"Daisy, you don't want that food do you?"

She looked down at the bag. "That's not food. I hate that stuff. What's wrong with you?"

"Well, if you don't want it, can I have it?"

A pair of teary blue eyes glowered at him, she shrugged, huffed out her breath and moved to thrust the bag in his direction.

"No! Don't throw it to me!" He wiggled his arms to remind her he was tied. Daisy rolled her eyes at him.

"Well, I can't spoon feed you from here. I can't reach, stupid, and besides, I think I'd rather you starve."

"Just, please, open the bag and take out the food. Humour me, okay?"

She looked at him as if he had lost his mind, but she did as he asked and pulled out a small container of fries and a wrapped burger, placing them on the flattened bag in front of her.

"Can you unwrap the burger?"

Daisy gave him another look but unwrapped the burger, carefully and deliberately lining it up on the bag and patting the top of the bun into place with sarcastic fingers.

"Okay, slide it over to me." The bag didn't slide well on the dirt floor, but Daisy had enough pent-up anger to send it a good metre past Peter's feet.

"Are there any other requests? Should I heat it for you, too?"

CHAPTER FOURTEEN

It wasn't long before there was a clatter from the rear corner of the barn.

"Quietly!" Peter hissed.

From her corner, Daisy gave him a look that was half disgust and half questioning. In reply, he nodded at the Dinglemen, who were now making a beeline across the floor towards the burger and fries.

"Hello, Peter, you called?" Sarge asked, keeping his gaze on the food.

"Why can't we use the door anymore?" complained Clever to the room in general. "What's wrong with a little sophistication?"

"Fries! My favourite." Nimin dashed across the floor and dived into the top of the container, sending up a spray of potato and salt.

Sarge and Clever both spied the gaping

Daisy at the same time and pulled up short to stare at Peter.

"We thought you must be alone!"

"She's seen us!"

"What were you thinking? And why are you sitting there?"

"I'm sorry, guys, but I'm tied to the chair. They caught me looking into the barn. Can you please try to get these ropes undone?"

"Peter? What are—" said Daisy.

Weebit stepped in front of Daisy and bowed low at the waist.

"Hello, fair young maiden."

Peter snorted and earned a glare from Daisy, despite her shock.

"My name is Weebit." He bowed low again. "I shall be your rescuer this warm, fine evening. I am most charmed to meet you and would very much like—" Weebit moved closer to her and indicated for Daisy to pick him up. She complied, and he continued to speak sweet nothings while Daisy's astonished face took on a dopey look of adoration.

"How does he do that?" asked Peter.

Sarge and Clever both pulled on the knots at his feet. It wasn't easy going. The rope was thick and Boggs had done a good job of making sure he couldn't move his legs. The last knot finally loosened and Clever lost his balance to sprawl backward onto the hard-packed dirt floor. He sprang to his feet, picked hay off his now less-than-pristine tunic, brushed dust off his leggings, and scowled at Sarge for not even trying to catch him. Sarge was too busy moving the length of rope, but suddenly paused, tilted his head and held up a hand. A few seconds later, Peter could hear a car approaching, pull into the yard and stop just outside the barn door.

"Hurry, Sarge!" said Peter.

Weebit was calming Daisy but she had heard the car and her face spoke volumes. Peter didn't think he had ever seen someone look so scared. Sarge quickly scaled a back leg of the chair, and then Peter could feel him tugging on the knots at his wrists. Another vehicle pulled into the yard, the engine cut and a door slammed. Peter sent a puzzled look at Daisy. She shook her head, she didn't know who was out there, either, but she didn't look as if she thought their arrival was a good thing. It didn't feel like Sarge was having much luck with the knot. It *felt* like he was using it as a canyon swing. Peter could hear muttered swearing and a low, bitter complaint from behind, something about troublesome humans who couldn't do anything right. Peter looked down to discover that the other Dinglemen had already disappeared, and he hadn't even detected them go. The barn door slid open and Peter squinted to see the man – no, men – who were framed in the doorway.

The first man flicked a light switch that was beside the door and the single weak globe cast enough light for Peter to see who entered. The man stepped forward to get a look at the captives, allowing another stranger, and then Boggs and Durdle, to cram in and fan out behind him. Boggs and Durdle both stared at Daisy, exchanged glances, stared again. The first man was wearing slacks and boat shoes and a yellow designer V-neck sweater. Peter noticed pocked cheeks, a thin nose and hair so black it looked dyed.

"That's not Smythe's daughter. He's been here," said Boggs.

Four pairs of cold eyes considered Daisy, who squeezed her knees close into her chest.

"I'm disappointed," said the first man, looking from Daisy to Peter, and shaking his head at the workmen. "Very disappointed.

Two kids, and neither the one I wanted? We were right not to trust Smythe. No more errors, do you understand me?" He kept his voice low but it was full of promised misfortune.

Peter glanced at Boggs, who nodded stiffly but kept his gaze on the floor. Behind him, Durdle looked straight ahead, apparently fascinated by a spot on the back wall. It felt to Peter as if Sarge had given up on swinging on the rope and was kicking him in the back instead. Peter was doing his best not to show any expression but a sharp dig in the kidneys made him grimace. The man with the thin nose narrowed his eyes and watched Peter until Daisy shifted uncomfortably, catching his attention as she scuffed the ground with her heels.

Peter glanced at the other stranger. A small, narrow-shouldered man who looked all wiry muscle. He wore black jeans with a dark blazer and sneakers, the jeans too large for him and cinched at his waist by a leather belt. He was a younger man than the first, maybe in his thirties, and Peter guessed he was second in command or maybe hired help. Peter received another kick in the back from a struggling Sarge and squirmed in his chair, trying his best not to move the rope that was only just lying across his ankles. If anyone noticed the rope was untied—

And then Peter realised it probably made no difference. It was too late. The thin-nosed man turned to Boggs and Durdle and spoke.

"We will deal with Smythe when we are done here. Go get blankets, shovels and torches. We are going to take these kids for a little walk into the bush."

Peter's mind raced but he couldn't think straight. Sarge had only loosened the knots at his hands, and although the men would have to untie him from the chair he didn't think he had much chance to escape or fight. Even with the Dinglemen's help, he didn't see how he could overpower four grown men. He tested the knot at his wrists anyway. It gave a little but not enough. His hands felt swollen and his fingers wouldn't work properly. Nobody knew where they were. He glanced over at Daisy but she wouldn't look up, her shoulders hunched and quivering and her face hidden by falling strands of hair. Peter's mind wandered to the club and to home. His Mum and Dad wouldn't know what happened to him. He swallowed and forced himself not to panic.

#

From behind the blue fluffy pillow on the bed, Clever watched Boggs and Durdle leave the barn on their errand. He could see Sarge still working hard to loosen the knots at Peter's wrists, but Sarge seemed to be having trouble because he couldn't get a firm foothold. Nimin was hunkered down beside Clever, watching the room with huge eyes and still licking salt off his fingers. Clever couldn't see Weebit but guessed he was somewhere near Daisy – somewhere he could comfort her without any other human in the room ever knowing.

An engine roared to life outside, making the new humans look at each other in surprise. The smaller of the two poked his head out of the barn door.

"Those two have bolted. You think the police are on their way? Something must have set them off."

Clever could see Peter moving his fingers to release the knot at his wrists, trying desperately to help Sarge untie him. Clever recognised the sound of the engine as the Hold-On roared away down the driveway. The boss human didn't seem too perturbed. He casually pulled a firegun from a pouch near his ankle and sauntered over to stand behind Peter, who immediately froze his hands.

"Go check," he ordered.

The small man went out. He was only gone a few minutes before he was back in the barn.

"Yes, the police are on their way. They got a tip-off."

Clever watched the boss human, who was still standing behind Peter, the firegun pressed into Peter's neck. He couldn't see Sarge anymore and hoped he was in a spot where he could help. And where was Weebit?

Just then, Weebit joined Clever and Nimin behind the pillow and nodded at Clever who took his point. It was time they armed themselves for a yike.

#

The boss leaned close to Peter's ear to whisper.

"Lucky for you. No point in killing you now. That would just make this whole farce even messier, so we'll just leave quietly—"

He suddenly screamed, hot breath on Peter's ear, before he doubled up in agony and thudded onto the ground. Peter swivelled his head as much as he could, to see the man in the foetal position, his hands grasping his groin. Under his grip, it looked as if an irritated rat was doing a rain dance on his privates. The boss screamed again and the voices of the Dinglemen joined in with a battle cry.

"*GAAARRHHH!*"

Clever, Nimin and Weebit all swarmed across the floor towards the younger man, who had stepped around Peter to stare in surprise at his prostrate boss. Hay was sticking out from all over their green clothes and hair, their faces were re-blackened and they had found weapons of a sort. Fish hooks. The man just stared in shock at the tiny swarming figures. That is, until they leapt onto his sneakers and disappeared from view under the hems of his jeans. A few seconds later and he'd dropped his gun, his yelps had joined his boss's and he danced on the spot, slapping wildly at his lower legs.

Peter attacked the knot at his wrists again and felt it finally start to give. He managed to slip one hand out from under the ropes and quickly brought his arms forward to yank the rope off completely. His shoulders complained at the movement. He bounded off the chair, grabbed the end of the rope, and scrutinised the boss who had turned white and looked as if he was going to faint.

Peter plucked the first of the man's hands from his crotch and looped the rope around his wrist, not exactly surprised when Sarge crawled out from the man's fly and glared at him.

"What happens in battle stays on the battlefield. Got it?" said Sarge, narrowing his eyes.

Peter bit his lip and nodded.

"Good."

Sarge spied the dancing man. "They started without me! Well, I can fix that." He cast one last steely gaze at Peter, reminded him, "not a word," and rushed off to join the others.

Peter finished tying up the boss and glanced over to see how the Dinglemen were doing. The second man looked as if he was in trouble. His jeans had rips in them from the fish hooks and the Dinglemen had managed to draw blood in several places. Sarge was clambering up the fabric on his back with a determined look on his face, and the man was still slapping and grabbing at himself, having no luck in stopping the barrage of hooks. Despite this, though, he had summed up his boss's situation and was making his way towards the doorway. Peter lunged for one of the guns and fired a shot off, loosening a fine shower of dust from the roof.

"Stop!"

The man and the Dinglemen stopped.

"Clever, can you get some more rope?" asked Peter, waving a wobbling gun at the man. In response, the man, while no longer walking away, started to smile. Confused, Peter blinked, and then he suddenly felt movement behind him. Before he could turn around another gun fired.

Daisy gripped the trembling gun between white-knuckled hands, her tear-streaked face working and her breath coming in gasps. She had fired at the boss, who, Peter now saw, had managed to get to his feet and move up close behind him, and it must have been a near shot. A large hole had opened up in the wall opposite. Daisy gulped and wiggled the gun, and the boss, most likely afraid of beginners' luck, carefully sat back down and allowed Peter to bind his feet with the rope. Peter realised then that he had tied the man with his hands to the front.

The younger man hadn't moved. He didn't want to get shot, either, and Daisy was looking unhinged. She waved the gun at the chair and he sat to be tied up by Peter, who then wobbled on unsteady legs to Daisy, gently took the gun from her and slumped down beside her. The Dinglemen looked unhappy that the fun was all over, but Weebit did come back over to stay with "his maiden warrior". Both men were staring open-mouthed at the Dinglemen, and Sarge looked from one to the other, grinning nastily.

"What?" he asked.

#

They could hear sirens coming. It wasn't long before police vehicles had screamed into the yard with strobing lights and sirens wailing, and soon there were blue uniforms milling all over the property.

The evening had become dark enough for a few stars to have appeared above them, but it was hard to see beyond all the lights flashing from the cars crammed into the yard. An ambulance trundled up the rough track, and Daisy and Peter were led over to it to be checked out by a paramedic. They were wrapped in blankets, handed flimsy plastic cups of lukewarm cocoa and generally fussed over.

The men had been led to different police cars, jammed into the rear seats and driven away, while another couple of cars pulled into the yard, and Daisy's and Peter's parents tumbled out to run over. Amid hugs, and threats if he ever did something like this again, Peter was wondering about the Dinglemen. With all of these people milling around, he thought it might be hard for them to get to him. He removed himself from his parents' arms and said he would just walk around a bit if that was okay, just to get a bit of air. They nodded reluctantly and he felt their eyes on his back as he walked away. Knowing that his aimless roaming must look a bit odd, he couldn't help smiling. He strolled past the barn, along the front of the orchard, and meandered towards the farmhouse, until he heard a pointed 'ahem'. He sat on the verandah for a minute, stood, and wandered back to his parents with four passengers riding underneath the blanket.

"Let's go home."

CHAPTER FIFTEEN

It was a few days later. Peter was seated in his usual spot in the clubroom kitchen, a cold can of lemonade dribbling a wet ring on the table in front of him. He was feeling content to just sit there and relax, taking a break from working on the driving range. Daisy was seated across from him and didn't appear to have been affected much by her recent experience. If anything, it seemed to have made her resolve to fix the world stronger, starting with the golfers. So far, she had already lectured two of them on their diets and disciplined a guy for wasting water. Caitlin looked as if she couldn't decide if she was glad to have her little sister back in one piece or if she wanted to throttle her. Mostly the latter.

Daisy had admitted to being the other saboteur. She couldn't stand by and see the woods torn down and all the wildlife left homeless or killed. The guard dog had stopped her from disabling the bulldozer the night before, so she had returned with some laced meat to put the dog to sleep, and had been passing the office door when she had been surprised by Mr Smythe. She had tried to run, but he had caught her and bundled her into the back of the Mercedes with her hands and feet bound. Mr Smythe had received a call on his mobile from his hysterical wife about the missing Camilla and he had circled back to the clubrooms. Peter kept quiet, but it occurred to him that he had been in Mr Smythe's office when she was tied up outside in the Mercedes.

There was a tentative knock against the door-jamb and Constable Denton, the young policeman who had interviewed Peter at the station, popped his head around to look into the kitchen. He glanced briefly at Peter and Daisy and grinned at Caitlin.

"Hi, ah, hello there. Do you mind if I join you?" He removed his cap and stood awkwardly in the doorway, twisting the blue material in his hands. This was the second visit by the constable in as many days, and Peter knew it was only because he was sweet on Caitlin.

"Coffee?" asked Caitlin. She raced to get another mug and indicated for the constable to sit at the top of the table.

"Thanks. White and one, please."

"Yes, I remember." Caitlin turned and smiled at him.

Daisy was looking at her older sister with a smirk on her face, and Peter saw the warning glare Caitlin threw at her.

"So, um, I just thought I'd drop in to see that you are both okay? Not suffering any delayed reactions or anything?"

Peter and Daisy raised sceptical eyebrows at him and he blushed furiously before clearing his throat. "Well, um, you both seem okay. So that's good, eh?"

Caitlin delivered his coffee and a plate of chocolate biscuits. Chocolate, Peter noted, not the boring plain ones she usually reserved for visitors. The constable smiled his thanks and just beat Peter's hand to the plate.

"I didn't get to tell you yesterday, we have some good news about Smythe," Constable

Denton continued. "He's been apprehended and is telling us everything. We'll have enough to put them all away for a long time." It turned out the police had been suspicious of Mr Smythe after receiving information that he was involved with the money laundering.

"That's why I put you off, Peter. We didn't want you getting mixed up with these men. You were both very lucky that we received the tip-off about your whereabouts."

Peter wondered if it had been Durdle who had called the police.

"Anyone else at the club involved, do you think?" asked Daisy.

"We're still interviewing, but no, we don't think the Board members knew anything."

"Why did the workmen kidnap Camilla?"

"Leverage over Smythe, we think, because of all the delays at the worksite. His partners thought he was up to something and wanted to put some pressure on him."

"And what about the workmen?" asked Peter.

"They've both been picked up." The constable shrugged and slurped at his coffee. Then he remembered something else. "Oh yeah, you guys will love this part. Apparently, our detainees are claiming to have been attacked by tiny little men!" He laughed and took another sip of coffee. He held his hand up, holding his index finger and thumb about six centimetres apart. "About this size. Tiny little men. With hooks for hands and razor sharp teeth. And that you, Peter, were talking to them! Can't you just picture it?" He shook his head. "Classic!"

"I didn't know you could get off kidnapping charges by pleading insanity," said Caitlin, joining in with a smile of her own.

Peter and Daisy just glanced at each other. Peter took a sip of his lemonade, demolished another chocolate biscuit and sighed happily. The best thing about all this? The woods were safe. The development was off. In fact, if anyone even mentioned the word 'resort' at the moment, the golfers just mumbled in embarrassment, and said they liked the trees and who needs more buildings mucking up their golf course? Things were really looking up. Best of all, the Dinglemen were staying. He really couldn't imagine his life without them, now that he had met them.

#

Clever was back to his favourite pastime – his research. Peter might be a friend, but that didn't mean he wasn't a good test subject. In fact, he was the perfect test subject. Clever was safe to follow him as closely as he pleased and even if he was noticed, which was unlikely, it wouldn't matter. He could just say 'hello' and resume observations at a later date. He knew Peter was going to be working near the fishes pond again this morning, clearing the overgrown greenery surrounding the water, so he headed purposefully through the trees in that direction. And even better, he thought, he now had a female subject for close observation as well. Peter and Daisy had become good friends since the barn and he was excited about monitoring them both together. He popped out of the woods, spied Peter bending over on the other side of the pond with a wheelbarrow parked beside him, and motored closer to his target. Clever had found he could easily get within a few feet of Peter without him knowing he was being observed.

Clever settled into a convenient position and commenced taking mental notes. The subject was singing again. Why does the subject sing sometimes when he is working and not at other times? Clever deduced the singing was a positive behaviour, but why did the subject do it? And couldn't he hear how terrible he sounded? Fortunately, the singing only appeared to happen when the subject thought he was alone. Does it mean the subject is happy? Content? The work is enjoyable? More importantly, Clever wondered, wincing at a particularly flat note, is the singing preventable?

Clever was also looking forward to watching his test subject interacting with other humans – his parents at home, with the golfers, with friends, with strangers. Possibly even hitch a ride to the education centre, the 'school', with Peter, which was supposed to be starting again soon. Peter wouldn't mind taking him, he was sure. Actually, the more Clever thought about this idea the more excited he felt. How much could he learn about humans in a place with the sole purpose of *learning*?

Clever sighed contentedly. He looked forward to more enjoyable afternoons of watching his subjects. He had been reminding himself all day that they were going to stay in the woods. They were going to stay in this Dingledell, where he would be able to sit out on the balcony and watch the birds flit by. Tomorrow, they were going back to the forest to collect the others, and he couldn't wait to bring them back here. He was sure the elders would be pleased and would cover him with praise. Well, maybe not. He wouldn't have been able to do it alone, he conceded, and the others would be celebrated along with him. And that was okay, because he was still the leader. He grinned to himself.

#

Peter stopped singing and straightened up when he saw Daisy walking towards him, carrying a brown paper bag and a water bottle.

"A cheese sandwich from the kitchen," she said, tossing him the bag.

"Thanks. I'm nearly done here anyway. Give me a moment to pack up my stuff and I'll walk back to the clubhouse with you."

They walked along the side of the fairways, mostly in companionable silence because Daisy was thinking about what had happened to them in the last few days and Peter had his mouth full of bread and cheese.

"So, the Dinglemen are going back to where they came from to bring others?" asked Daisy

"Yep."

"How long do you think they'll be gone? I'll miss them."

"Yeah, hopefully not long. I can't picture this place without them either."

"Sometimes I can't believe what's happened this summer."

"I can't believe we have school next week."

"True, hard to believe." Daisy nodded.

They both fell silent again, each lost in their own thoughts.

#

Larry Cleghorn, the lorry driver, grumbled miserably. He shouldn't be working today. The company just didn't employ enough drivers to cover his run up to the forest. He sniffed painfully, whooshed out his breath in a cloud of throat lozenge vapour and glared at the road ahead. He blinked gritty eyes, rubbed his sleeve under his nose and hunched over the steering wheel.

Well ahead of the lorry, someone on a bike wobbled pathetically into the road, arms and legs flailing as the bike gave up on balance and fell over. The person crunched awkwardly onto the tarmac and lay prone in the middle of the road. Normally, Larry would have been able to stop in ample time, but his reflexes were slowed by his stuffy head. He only just managed to haul the lorry to a squealing halt before hitting either person or bike, and it was a close thing with the bike. He whooshed out his breath again, this time in a mix of relief and rage, before swinging down to yell at the figure in the road.

"Hey, you clown! I nearly ran you over—" he rasped, interrupted by another painful coughing fit. The person turned over and Larry realised he was only a teenager, maybe fourteen at the most. Old enough to know better, thought Larry, angrily. He continued to rant at the boy about not watching what he was doing. The boy smiled an apology at him, picked himself up and slowly patted himself down for injuries. Larry didn't think the boy looked that upset about falling off his bike. The only time he grimaced was when his patting fingers located a small tear near the hem of his black tee shirt. The boy finally looked up and shrugged another apology to Larry, and then sauntered over to pick up the bike. Larry fell silent. His ranting seemed to be falling on deaf ears, anyway, so what was the point?

Larry sniffed again, groaned wretchedly, and climbed back into the lorry, feeling even sorrier for himself as he turned the key in the ignition and set off once again towards his destination. One last grumpy glance in the rear view mirror made his blood boil. The boy was standing on the curb with a small blonde girl. Where had she come from? He shook his head in disgust and then winced at his aggravated headache. Kids these days had no respect, he thought bitterly. They must have been playing games, the cheek! Otherwise, why would they be grinning and waving cheerily to the back of his lorry?

www.ingramcontent.com/pod-product-compliance
Lightning Source LLC
Chambersburg PA
CBHW051420170626
46809CB00006B/2255